Stories of Faith
Discover the Power of Faith

RL Literary productions

Introduction

Chapter eleven of the Book of Hebrews provides the following definition for faith:

"Faith is confidence in what we hope for and assurance about what we do not see."

At first glance, it may seem something distant and unconnected with everyday life, but if we reflect a little bit, we will see faith in the smallest details.

A person sets their alarm believing they will be alive the next day. Someone who is sick believes that they will get better and be cured. In general, people believe the future will be better; they believe the crisis and struggles will be overcome. Even if there is no evidence, there is faith.

Faith is even more powerful when it is supported by God and his power. The one who trusts believes that all things are possible, believes that everything will always be better, and believes that God is always in their path, no matter the situation they are facing.

Genuine faith sees no difficulties, impediments, obstacles, or impossibilities. Jesus Christ himself said that all things are possible to the one who believes. He did not say some things are possible, He said everything is possible. Furthermore, Jesus also said that with God all things are possible.

Combine these two certainties, and you will have the greatest power someone has ever dreamed of. All things will be possible with your faith and God's help.

Table of Contents

I Can't Believe

The experienced doctor Alberto Calixto was impressed about what he was seeing. That seemed impossible to happen; in all his twenty years of oncology, he had never witnessed anything like that.

"I can't continue!" he exclaimed in surprise to the surgical team.

"Why?" asked his assistant.

"There are no tumors here!"

"What?" the assistant was surprised. "All the exams showed tumors."

"I know what the exams have shown."

Alberto walked towards some monitors where image exams were. He looked attentively at them. The images were unquestionable; there were tumors in the patient's abdomen. However, the reality was totally the opposite.

The patient's abdomen was open, and there was no sign that one day he had a tumor. All his organs were plenty healthy.

"Let's close him," Alberto said. "I think I know what happened here…"

Alberto was assisting that patient, a middle-aged man, for a few months.

At the first medical appointment, Alberto noticed the man was confident and had a contagious smile.

"Good morning, doctor!" the man said with excitement.

"Good morning, André," the doctor replied seriously.

"How about your day? Are you having a good day?" André continued in the same enthusiastic tone.

Alberto sighed and said, discouraged, "André, I'm an oncologist. How can I have a good day?"

"I know your work can seem hard and sad. But you can introduce the patients to a new treatment and give them hope. You may say a better diagnosis than the patient was hoping. And things like that."

"Maybe," Alberto replied, discouraged.

"What are the pieces of news for me?"

"André, unfortunately, I don't have good news," replied uncomfortably.

"What happened? Weren't my exams as expected?"

"Your exams confirmed the suspicions of the doctor who referred you to an oncologist. You have some tumors in your abdomen."

"Oh, my God!" André was amazed. "And now, what I'll do?"

"You'll start chemotherapy."

"Will it be effective?"

"This treatment is effective in cases like yours."

"Thank God!" André replied excitedly, "And also thank the doctor and the medicines," he smiled.

"Do you believe in God?"

"Of course! You don't?"

"I don't believe in God."

"Doctor, you should be the first one to believe."

"Why?"

"You studied the human body, its functions, systems, cells, and everything else. You know and see the perfection of each of us. You can see God's work more than the others."

"Perhaps it's because of it that I don't believe. I see how and why everything is working. I can explain most things."

"But this it's not a reason to disbelieve in God. We can explain how too many things work; however, this doesn't mean we can't believe in God. We can see his action upon everything and understand how it works too."

"This is an interesting point of view. But let's talk about your treatment."

"Alright."

Alberto explained all the details to André. The patient was attentive to all the doctor's words. As soon as he had some doubt, he asked. The doctor was very polite and replied to each of his doubts.

After all the explanations, Alberto said, "Are you ready for the treatment?"

"I have to be ready!" André replied confidently, "I'll overcome this sickness with God's help."

"Do you really believe that God can help you?"

"I do."

"Why?"

"Because I know God. He never put his children to shame. He never lets his children perish."

"If that's true, why do you have cancer?"

Alberto was testing André's faith.

"God always has a purpose in all things. Now, I don't know why. If God wants, he'll show me the reason. If he doesn't, it's alright. I trust in him." André replied, assured because he had no doubts about God's plan.

All these believers say the same thing. I think these words comfort them in the face of the tragedy of cancer. Alberto thought.

The doctor replied, "I see you're a man of faith."

He smiled and said, "Maybe the doctor can come to my side."

"It would take something extremely unusual to change my

mind," Alberto replied, seriously.

"There's nothing impossible to God!"

They talked about other treatment details, and so they said goodbye.

Alberto continued his medical appointments. The next one was a young lady with breast cancer. Her treatment was at an advanced stage, and she was weak due to the side effects of chemotherapy.

He had done his best to stop the growth of the tumors, but until that moment, he only got to slow them down.

He always gave her the same report and noticed her sadness.

She entered the room wearing a headscarf to hide her lack of hair. She was pale and used makeup to disguise her sick appearance.

"Good morning, Patrícia."

"Good morning, doctor," she replied in a low voice, almost whispering.

"How are you today?"

"I'm feeling weak."

"It's a side effect of the treatment."

"I know. This treatment is taking so long," said discouraged, "I'm tired."

"Let's see how your exams are."

Alberto looked at his monitor and read the medical report, "The tumors show a subtle decrease compared to the last analysis."

He would give her the news in his usual tone; however, he remembered André's words, "You can say a better diagnosis than the patient was hoping."

The doctor changed his mind and tried to say positively, "Patrícia, we have good news! The tumors started to decrease; the treatment was efficient!"

She gave a faint smile and said with excitement, "For real? I can't believe it!"

"You can believe it. Your tumors are decreasing."

She cried with joy and said, "I was so discouraged about this treatment. I couldn't see the light at the end of the tunnel. I confess that I was thinking about giving up."

Oh, no! He thought and remembered André's words, "Give them hope."

"Patrícia," he said seriously and confidently, "you can't give up. You must go ahead to get well. It's the only way."

"I know it, doctor," she replied while drying her tears, "but I'm sure the doctor knows better than anyone how hard the treatment is. It's an endless suffering."

"I know it."

"This fresh news cheers me up," she said confidently, "I'll continue the treatment until I get healed."

"That's the spirit!" he replied excitedly.

Why did I say this? Alberto was confused about his words. *I talked to that patient once, and is he influencing me? What's happening here?*

Patrícia noticed that he was lost in his thoughts and said, "Doctor? Are you okay?"

He came to his senses and replied, "I'm fine. I was thinking about the next steps of your treatment."

"Alright."

"Patrícia, you'll keep the same medicine as before…"

He explained to her what would be done.

André came back home and went to the living room. He sat on the sofa and leafed through a Holy Bible. He stopped in the text, "So do not fear, for I am with you; do not be dismayed, for I am your God. I will strengthen you and help you; I will uphold you with my righteous right hand." Isaiah 41:10.

He sighed and said, "Oh Lord, I don't know why I'm facing this cancer, but the Lord does. I trust in the Lord and his promise. I know that in all things the Lord works for the good of those who love you. I'm sure that if the Lord wants, I'll be healed and restored. The Lord has the final saying and the definitive diagnostic. I believe even in a sad situation like that, the Lord is in control."

A few days later, André started the treatment in the hospital. He had to go there some days of the week.

He always talked to other patients about faith, hope, encouragement, and everything each person needed to hear. He never seemed to be sad or discouraged.

Alberto noticed his attitude and went to the chemotherapy room to talk to André. The doctor was sitting beside him.

"André, I'm curious about you and all you're doing."

"Am I doing something wrong or forbidden?"

"Don't. However, you're not reacting as most of the patients. You're always in high spirits, excited, in a good mood."

André smiled.

"The doctor hoped I would be sad and upset, wouldn't you?"

"This is the usual behavior," replied constrained.

"Doctor, think with me. What If I get upset, sad, hopeless, and full of negative feelings? Would this improve my health?"

"Of course, it wouldn't."

"The battle against the tumor is hard, and I need to do my best to win it. A soldier can't go to war thinking how dangerous it is, how many risks he will face, or how strong the enemy is.

He must face everything bravely and without fear. I'm doing the same thing."

Some studies indicate better efficacy in the treatment of those who keep a positive attitude. Alberto thought.

"That makes sense," he agreed, "and how about your beliefs? Do they keep as strong as last time we talked?"

"Of course, they are stronger than ever!" André stated, convinced, "I believe that God is always with me, no matter what I'm facing."

He's a character, even though he lives in a terrible situation; he thinks God is with him. Believers... The doctor thought.

"That's good," Alberto said this to avoid a discussion. He had already noticed that André was very confident in God, and nothing would change his mind.

"Doctor, how long will you know about the efficacy of chemotherapy?"

"About one month".

"Alright," André replied.

A nurse came to them and said something to Alberto. He got up and said, "I have to go. If you need anything, you can call a nurse or ask to talk to me."

"Thank you. God bless you, doctor."

"Okay."

The doctor went away, and André waited for the end of his session.

Alberto was at home having dinner with his wife, Ana.

"My love," he said, "I'm dealing with a new situation, and I need your opinion."

"What's happening?"

"I'm assisting a patient with multiple tumors, and he seems very confident about God's help in his life."

"What opinion do you wanna? Of a psychiatrist or my opinion as a believer?"

"Both of them."

"Well, as a psychiatrist, the patient is leaning on something bigger than him, God. His faith helps him to have a positive view of this situation. Tumors are severe and can make anyone tremble. He's using a defense mechanism to keep calm and hopeful."

"And your opinion as a believer."

"God can do everything, and there is no reason to fear. Everything has a purpose, even if we don't understand it."

"You talked like him," he smiled.

"All believers talk in the same way, didn't you notice?" she smiled.

"Yes, I did."

"Don't forget that you were a believer too."

He sighed and said, discouraged, "Yes, I was…"

Alberto was a teenager. He, his parents, and his younger brother traveled in a car.

The father was driving, and his brother said, "Are we there yet?"

"Diego!" said Alberto, a bit nervous, "you've asked the same thing ten minutes ago. We'll know when we arrive."

"I can't wait to arrive at the beach!" Diego exclaimed excitedly. "I love the sea!"

"All of us love the sea!" replied the mother, "But we have to be patient till we arrive there."

"Oh, my God!" yelled the father desperately.

He pulled the car off the road abruptly, making the tires screech on the asphalt. The family got scared, and the boys cried out.

"What happened?" the mother asked.

He was panting and said, "A crazy one invaded our lane and almost hit us."

"Jesus!" she was astonished, "I didn't see anything!"

"Everything happened too fast to notice!"

"God delivered us from death," said Alberto, "let's thank his blessings."

They closed their eyes, and Alberto prayed, "Dear God, thank you for protecting our lives. We thank everything you do for us. Lord, continue blessing and protecting us during this trip. I pray in Jesus' name."

"Amen", everyone replied.

They continued the trip and arrived at a stunning beach with crystal water and white sand.

After some days of enjoying the beach, the family went on a boat trip. They visited other beaches and close islands in a small yacht.

The morning was sunny and hot, but in the afternoon, the sky darkened with dense clouds. As the boat was returning, the rain started to fall. At first, it was only a gentle shower that did not disturb the calm sea. Nobody in the boat was concerned about it. The only thing that everyone made was putting life jackets on.

The wind and rain got stronger; the waves grew up and shook the boat violently; like they were inside a blender. Lightning ripped across the sky, and the crush of thunder created the perfect storm. Alberto's family hugged themselves in a corner of the boat and prayed with all their hearts. All of them were desperate and fearful.

The boat's captain could hardly navigate because of the

huge waves. They hit the boat filling it with water. The boys cried because they feared their destiny, and the parents tried to comfort them.

At one point, a wall of water struck the boat with all its strength and impetus. The yacht did not resist and capsized. The passengers were thrown into that implacable sea.

Alberto was separated from his family. He shouted their names, but nobody replied. In his last effort, he yelled, "God, please, save my family!"

Alberto stayed adrift and lonely. The waves tossed him around like a rag doll. He could see the boat slowly sinking, and his family clinging to the wreckage. He tried to swim towards them, but the waves were too strong.

Suddenly, a giant wave crashed over him, and he lost consciousness. When he woke up, he was floating on his back, looking up at the sky. The storm was still raging, and the family was nowhere to be seen.

The storm raged on for hours, and a rescue team found Alberto. He desperately begged them to search for his family. The search led them to nothing, but he did not want to give up. The rescuers sedated him and led him to the city.

The next day, Alberto was in a hospital room, and there was a television was turned on. A female journalist said, "The Coast

Guard is searching for the victims of yesterday's shipwreck. Some bodies have been found, and the authorities believe there are no survivors."

Images of bodies rescued were exhibited, and Alberto got desperate when he recognized his father's clothes. Tears filled his eyes, and he cried, "Dad!"

Alberto was the only survivor of that tragedy; his family and faith died together.

After some weeks of chemotherapy, André was suffering its side effects. He was pale, bald, and thin. He was in a medical appointment with Alberto.

"André," said sadly, "unfortunately, I don't have good news. Chemotherapy has no effect; your tumors are bigger than before."

"No big deal," André replied in the usual tone; he showed no sadness.

The doctor was amazed about André's reply and said, "Did you understand your situation?"

"Yes, I did it."

"How can you stay so calm?"

"Doctor," said firmly, "everything is under God's control. He has the final say about my health. If he wants, all can change quickly."

Here we go again with this speech about faith and God. Alberto thought.

"I know the doctor can't comprehend my words and feelings," André continued, "don't worry; everything will happen according to God's will."

"You're right, I can't comprehend you."

"What are the next steps in my treatment?"

"You'll use stronger medicines and more sessions of chemotherapy. I believe this will have better results."

"Alright. What if there are no better results?"

"The only option will be surgery."

"Let's start new chemotherapy, and then we think about the future. I don't wanna have more preoccupations besides what I already have."

"This is a good attitude. One thing at a time."

André continued his treatment, and whenever he could, he talked to the patients about faith, God, and better days. Gradually, many of the patients were changing their minds.

They have been influenced by André and faced that situation from another perspective. Some of them did not believe in divine intervention or miracles yet; however, they found hope in facing their sicknesses.

The doctor always observed André's behavior at the

hospital. And he frequently thought that his presence was positive for that room. Before him, there was a place of sadness, disillusion, fear, and negativity. But since André started his treatment, the room became a place of support, hope, encouragement, and will to live.

Alberto noticed that all his patients showed improvement in their cases; tumors were decreasing, chemotherapy was most effective, and their appearance improved. He heard similar stories from other doctors.

Even Alberto had changed. He always remembered André's first words and tried to provide help and support to the patients; it did not matter what was the case; he used a positive approach, highlighting the benefits and chances of the treatment instead of the worst side.

Some weeks later, André was on another medical appointment. He was still more affected by chemotherapy side effects, but he did not lose his optimism and faith.

"André, your last exams indicated the tumors kept increasing. You'll need surgery."

"Doctor," replied with a hoarse and weak voice, "I suppose there are some risks, don't?"

"Yes, there are risks," Alberto answered hesitantly.

"Don't hesitate. You can say it frankly. I'm ready for

everything, even to die. If this happens, I'll go towards God. There's nothing to fear."

Wow! I've never seen this kind of certainty before. Alberto thought, impressed.

"Alright, André," he replied, "I'm gonna be honest with you."

Alberto explained to him all the details and risks, and these were many. André agreed to everything he had heard. During all that moment, he showed peace and confidence.

The doctor was amazed at his serenity.

There is something different in this man. I can't understand how he can keep the same expression before this situation. He thought.

Before the surgery, André had to map the tumors' positions. He underwent several advanced imaging exams. These indicated all the details of the tumors. Alberto elaborated a surgical plan based on the exams.

After the surprise in the surgery, Alberto closed André's abdomen and led him to the room.

Alberto reviewed all the exams, medical reports, images, annotations, and everything he had about that case. He could not believe what had happened.

"The exams were wrong," he reasoned with himself.

He compared all the exams and saw the same tumors in André's body. He read all the reports, and they agreed on the diagnosis. Alberto even checked the names of the doctors in charge of those exams. And to his astonishment, they were not the same doctors.

"It can't be!" he exclaimed in disbelief, "Different doctors saw the same thing at different moments. I'm sure I'm letting something go."

The doctor spent hours analyzing everything about André's case, and he led to nothing. He could not explain his miraculous recovery. Everything attested that André had tumors and needed surgery to remove them.

A female nurse knocked on his door.

"Please, get in!" he answered.

"Doctor, André woke up."

"I'm gonna talk to him. Thank you."

He went to the room and gaped at André. His appearance had changed; he was as vigorous and healthy as the first medical appointment. Alberto was so impressed that he froze for a while.

"Doctor," André called him, "are you okay?"

"I'm fine," replied, confused.

"How was my surgery?"

"This is the question. There was no surgery."

"No surgery?" asked amazed, "Why? Was there anything wrong with me? Were there any complications?"

"André," Alberto replied, seriously, "there was no tumor in your body. We interrupted the surgery as soon as we had opened your abdomen. And now, you seem better than the first time I saw you."

"Thanks to God!" André boomed.

"I don't know if it was God who did it."

André smiled and said, "I know the doctor knows that was him."

"I did my best to find out a reason or evidence of what happened, but I have no answers."

"The doctor has no logical answers. You know what happened, but you don't wanna admit it."

"Do I know?" he questioned surprised, "I don't know."

"Yes! You know!" André exclaimed, "You saw God's action."

"No way!" he replied emphatically, "I don't believe it!"

"You may not believe it, but it happened. Do you have any explanation?"

"I don't."

"Have you ever seen anything like that?"

"No, I haven't."

"So, we are before a miracle of God. Do you know what a miracle means?"

"I suppose it is something that has no logical explanation and that its action must be caused by a higher power."

André smiled and said, "You replied as a dictionary. In this case, the higher power is God, the Lord, the Creator of the world and the Universe."

"I don't know what to think," he replied doubtfully.

"You don't have to think; you have to believe in God."

"It's not so simple."

"Does the doctor remember what you said in our first appointment?"

"I'm sorry, but I don't remember."

"The doctor said you needed an extremely unusual thing to change your mind. Now, you've got it."

Alberto remembered his words and thought, *He's right; I really said this.*

André was looking attentively at Alberto, waiting for some answer.

The doctor sighed and said, discouraged, "I'm lost with all this. I suffered in my past when I believed in God, and I don't wanna live it all over again."

"God will give you a fresh start," stated confidently and

gently, "no matter what you've lived. The past doesn't matter; look ahead and accept a blessed future."

These words deeply moved Alberto's heart. He sat next to André's bed and said, "Please, talk more about this fresh start and blessed future."

André told Alberto some parts of his story and gave him many undeniable proofs that God had helped and led him in those situations. Alberto was amazed about all he heard, and a small flame of faith burned in his heart. Alberto reconsidered his belief in God for the first time in more than thirty years. On that day began a long and strong friendship based on faith. André helped the doctor with all his doubts until Alberto accepted God in his heart and life again.

The story of André's miraculous healing spread through the hospital, and many people went to him to hear about what he had experienced. Because of his testimony, many people believed in God: doctors, nurses, patients and their relatives, and other people.

André became a volunteer in the hospital. He always encouraged people to believe in God, have positive attitudes, and always do their best in all situations.

What am I doing wrong?

A middle-aged woman was sitting on a desk full of papers. Because of the poorly lit room, that task demanded more attention from her. She looked at the papers and wrote them down in a notebook.

With each paper she looked at, her expression became sadder. At one point, she threw everything on the table, scattering them everywhere, and sighed.

"Lord," said sadly, "I can't understand! Why am I here? I can't even pay all these bills! What's wrong? What am I doing wrong?"

She leaned her head on the desk and started crying.

"I thought I would make the difference!" said crying, "I suppose this place would be better without me."

The woman poured out before the Lord all her tears and sufferings. She had already held herself back for too long…

Some years ago, Simone had arrived in that small and forgotten town. Leontino was so far from the state capital, and consequently virtually abandoned by the authorities. Besides that, the region was very arid. The climate was desert-like, with average temperatures above one hundred Fahrenheit degrees.

All these ingredients created the perfect recipe for a

miserable environment. Everything around there exhaled poverty: unfinished clay houses, endless dust everywhere, skinny people and animals, dirty roads, and the icing on the cake, a sea of children. Each house had at least five of them. They formed a staircase when placed side by side. It was as if one was born every year.

Despite this chaotic scenario, Simone was optimistic about her job because she believed she could make a difference in the lives of the people of Leontino. She was sent by a Christian church in the state capital. Her church was already developing a job there. Some members visited the place for evangelistic purposes, and they took supplies to the town on each visit.

Because of the support, the church and its members were welcome there. All people did their best to assist them during the visits.

Simone visited that town sometimes and got touched about the situation. She was taken by a strong desire to aid them; everyone from that place was constantly on her mind. Simone cried, fasted, begged, and claimed help from God every day. Those people turned into her beloved ones.

After a few months of suffering, Simone was invited to a meeting with the church management.

"Simone," said a middle-aged woman, "you always showed

your wish to help people in Leontino; all of us are willing to do the same thing. Until now, we hadn't had a concrete opportunity. However, God opened a door for us."

"Tell me more about this opened door," Simone asked.

"Our church got the resources to send someone there full time," the woman continued, "your name was the first one in our minds."

"Was it because of my wish to help them?"

"Not only that. It was also because of your qualifications; you can work as a teacher. The church will pay you a wage and help with your needs. You'll help them improve their knowledge, and also it will evangelize them. What do you think?"

Simone was thrilled about that proposal and replied excitedly, "It would be like a dream coming true! I'll gather my two passions: teaching and evangelizing. When can I start?"

"We'll iron the last details out," replied a man, "I suppose that in some weeks everything will be ready."

"Some weeks?" she questioned in disbelief.

"I'd like to be quicker," replied the man, "but there are many things to do."

"I'm not upset about the delay!" exclaimed joyfully, "It's much less time than I expected. Glory to God!"

Simone was overjoyed about everything. She comprehended that opportunity as God's confirmation of her prayers.

They continued talking about other details of Simone's future mission. She heard everything attentively and excitedly.

This opportunity is all I ever wanted. She thought.

At the end of the meeting, they prayed to God for him to guarantee the success of that mission.

The next few days, Simone was filled with anxiety as she imagined how the trip would be, her work, people's reception, etc. She thanked God every moment and felt that this was her mission as a Christian.

Weeks later, her dream came true. She traveled to Leontino. The only way to get there was to travel by car because there was no airport near that town. It was an adventure until she arrived at her final destination. The first challenge was the traffic jam; she spent hours traveling a short distance and got enraged.

After almost two hours of quiet traffic, she was surprised again; it started a torrential rain on the road. Simone could hardly see three feet ahead of the car. She had to stop on the shoulder.

"Lord!" exclaimed concerned. "What's this rain? I've never seen anything like this. God, I beg you that this rain stops."

Simone stayed parked for almost an hour while the

floodgates of heaven were opened. She prayed the whole time.

The storm ceased, and the missionary Simone continued her travel. She was driving and praying fervently to God.

"Lord, bless my way, don't let anything disturb me. Protect me from all evils and troubles."

The next few hours were perfect, and she traveled more than half of her route. She got tired and stopped at a roadside restaurant. She had lunch and rested for a while. There was a television next to the exit, and she watched for an instant. A male journalist said, "A semi-truck crashed into several vehicles on highway two-one-three. Firemen did their best to save everyone, but some people didn't resist."

"Oh, my God!" she was amazed about the tragedy, "May God comfort the beloved ones."

"The crash was close to the city of Santana," continued the journalist, "about one in the afternoon."

Santana? One in the afternoon? This sounds familiar. She reasoned.

"Oh, Lord!" she said, frightened by what came to her mind, "I remembered when I heard these words."

Simone was at home packing her suitcases, and a young woman said, "I'm checking your route. You'll be close to Santana by one in the afternoon. You have to stop there!" she said excitedly.

"Why?"

"This city has the best corn-on-the-cob of the state! It's fantastic!"

Simone returned to her car, bowed her head, and prayed humbly, "Lord, thank you for your protection upon my life. If I hadn't had these delays, I could be a victim of that crash. Forgive my anger and my questioning at the beginning of the trip. I couldn't even imagine that could be good for me. May the Lord continue blessing me for the next few hours."

She stayed reflecting for some minutes and so, continued her path. Simone passed slowly through the place of the crash and was shocked by the sight of the destroyed vehicles and injured people. Vehicles and their parts were spread on the shoulders of the road; rescue teams were still assisting people; there were blood stains on the asphalt. The picture was terrifying.

Simone thanked God wholeheartedly when saw what could happen if she had made it as she planned. She could breathe a sigh of relief.

After some hours of driving, Simone finally arrived at Leontino. She went to the home of a local family whose members always supported the church on their visits. The missionary was welcomed and greeted by everyone she saw; all people were waiting anxiously for her presence.

In the next few days, she started preparing everything she needed for her missionary work. There were many things to do; however, there were also many people to help with all the tasks. Everyone in the town was willing to see that project on course. People worked hard to reform the building that would be the school; they did everything under Simone's guidance.

While they were working, Simone started another job; she was talking to the future students. The missionary met them and collected their information; she explained their student responsibilities and told them what she would teach.

After the building was reformed, the classes started. Simone divided the students according to their age and level of knowledge. She taught them in three shifts: morning, afternoon, and night.

The main subject of the classes was everything related to Portuguese: grammar, literature, text production and interpretation, etc. Occasionally, Simone taught basic mathematics and some history, geography, and science topics. She did her best to support them in their needs.

It was part of her mission to teach people using biblical texts. In this way, she could evangelize them and teach simultaneously. This method was working perfectly; the students were improving their scholarship skills and being evangelized. Simone analyzed biblical texts and contextualized them to the classes. All of them were able to understand the message of the text and identify the aspects related to Portuguese study.

After a few weeks, the results of her efforts were seen. Many students who had low grades were changing their situations. Their grades were improving, and the schools and families were recognizing them.

Simone was fulfilled about what was taking place. She felt as if she was leaving a positive mark on that town.

After weeping, Simone retook the papers and continued taking notes.

"I need to pay this quickly; this, I can delay the payment," she said while separating the bills.

The next day, she walked apprehensively along the city's main street, carefully observing everyone and everything. Most people looked with distrust and some anger. Simone was no longer welcome by a large part of the local population. She felt like a witch in the Middle Ages.

After a few months in Leontino, Simone already knew everyone, and they trusted her. Thus, there were no secrets in the conversations of the residents. One day, during the class break, two teenage girls were talking in the classroom while Simone was reading a book.

"Are you ready for the great day?" asked one of them excitedly.

"More or less," the girl replied, discouraged.

"Why?"

"I don't know if it's the right time," replied sadly.

"It's the perfect time!" the girl stated confidently, "you're at the perfect age to get married. Or do you think some man will want to marry you when you are older?"

Simone stopped her reading.

What? She thought, amazed. *Get married?*

The girl sighed and said, "I suppose you're right. It will be best for me to get married."

Simone could not keep silent and interrupted, "Girls, apologize for my intrusion, but are you talking about getting married for now?"

Simone walked towards them and sat.

"Yes, teacher," replied that one who was excited, "it's the custom here. Didn't you notice there are no single women in the town?"

Simone thought for a while and replied, "I had never

41

noticed, but I'm remembering all the women I've met, and they're all married."

The second girl replied, "Men here don't like old women. If a woman overpasses twenty, she will hardly get married. Men said she isn't attractive and wouldn't be a good wife."

Oh, my God! Simone thought in astonishment and asked, "What's your age?"

"Fifteen."

"And what's the age of your future husband?"

"Thirty-something."

"Holy moly!" Simone was so impressed that she boomed.

"Teacher?" They were surprised by her words.

"I'm sorry, but this is so strange for me."

"What's it like where you live?"

"Most of the people get married after twenty-something. And the ages are closer."

"I'd like people here to think like that," said the future bride.

"They don't, but I'll do something," Simone said confidently, "this thought about marriage is old-fashioned and illegal."

"Illegal?" The girls were surprised.

"Yes, it's illegal. In Brazil, the minimum age to marry is

sixteen, and the parents must formalize an authorization for the state authority."

"Hum…" the girl said discouraged, "this only works in big cities. Here, there is a party, and the couple goes to their home to live happily ever after," she said ironically.

"This is almost a prison!" Simone was exalted.

"It's the prison of all of us," replied the other girl.

"This will stop from now on! I promise you!" Simone said confidently.

"How?" they asked.

"You'll see it. Excuse me, I need to call someone."

Simone got up and left the classroom. The teenager ran after her, hugged her with tears, and said, "Teacher, thank you for taking care of me."

Simone hugged her tightly and replied, "I'll always do my best to care for everyone here."

After this touching moment, Simone called someone.

Days later, Simone gathered the entire town population in the main square. She had said that there would be a significant announcement for everyone.

Some strange people —men and women in formal wear— were on an elevated platform. Nobody had ever seen them before. They seemed influential people. A middle-aged woman took the microphone.

"Good morning, I'm Júlia, the state prosecutor, and I'm here with my tribunal coworkers to talk about a serious subject that arrived at us: underage marriages."

All the people looked at each other, and the woman continued, "What happens here cannot even be named marriage. It's almost kidnapping and rape!" she said reproachfully, "Teenagers are becoming wives and mothers. What century do you think you are in? Sixteenth? Seventeenth?"

Leontino's inhabitants were impressed by her speech.

"From now on," she continued firmly, "these abusive relationships are banished from this town. If any man takes a teenager as his wife, he'll be arrested and accused of being a rapist. I suppose that all of you know what happens to rapists in prison," said threateningly.

The men looked at each other, frightened.

A middle-aged man took the microphone.

"To guarantee what the prosecutor said, we'll set up a police station in the town. All women who feel threatened, harassed, coerced, or anything that upsets them can talk to us. We have police officers to hear and protect you."

Many women felt relieved hearing this. That seemed like a

small light amid dense darkness.

The people on the platform continued talking about what they would do for the people in Leontino. The female audience was thrilled about the promises, but the male audience felt like their reign had fallen.

As Simone expected, her attitude generated a malaise in the town. Several people saw her as an enemy, as she was destroying the social order and the "morals". They felt the outsider was trying to alter ancient traditions. Even with all disapproval and criticism, Simone continued her missionary work.

Law enforcement established themselves in the town and acted as they promised. Since that speech, there has been no underage marriage. Even some previous marriages were dissolved. The teenagers could turn into women and decide when they wanted to get married and if they would do it.

Coincidence or not, after these happenings, the church that supported Simone reduced her wage and financial help. She demanded some explanations, but they only replied that it was hard to get money. Despite having few resources, Simone kept doing her best for Leontino.

Sometime later, Simone visited the house of a family with many children, and the woman was pregnant. The missionary could not understand why they wanted a new baby living in that poor situation.

"Sandra," Simone was a little hesitant, "I'm curious about one thing. Can I ask you?"

"Yes, you can."

"My question is indiscreet. Why do you have so many children?"

"I'm gonna reply to you with another question. What can I do differently? How could I not have more children?"

"You could use condoms, contraceptives, IUD, tubal ligation, vasectomy, and there are still more ways to prevent pregnancy."

"Look at my situation," Sandra opened her arms to show her poor house. "How can I pay for this?"

"You don't need to pay; these methods are free and provided by the government. You only need to seek your rights."

"If I get it, I don't know if this is right," replied discouraged.

"Why wouldn't it be right?" Simone asked in surprise.

"What if God doesn't approve of avoiding babies? I learned that children are a gift from God."

"They are a gift. But God doesn't wanna see anybody suffering because of poverty and misery. We must do our part. If someone isn't able to sustain a baby, they must not have one. It's our personal choice."

Sandra reflected on Simone's words and said, "I think that makes sense. You should talk to all the women here because we all think the same."

"For real?"

"Yes, we don't know anything about our rights or what we can do to get them. I suppose that regarding the episode of underage marriages, you noticed how much the people here need information."

"That's true."

"And besides that, it's hard for good things to arrive at this place."

"It's hard but isn't impossible. And for God, all things are possible!" Simone exclaimed confidently.

Sandra smiled and said, "What will you do?"

"I'll make a call." Simone smiled.

"You have many influential contacts."

"Even though it may not seem like it, too many people are committed to doing the right thing and helping others."

"I'm glad you're here and are one of these people."

"And I'm glad I can be useful!"

They continued talking, and so, Simone went away and called someone.

Days later, Simone started to gather the women and talk to them about her new project. Some of them were resistant to the idea of birth control. But after the missionary highlighted the possibilities and advantages for them and their families, they seemed more open to it.

As expected, there was opposition to that new. Many people drastically opposed it, saying that Simone was against God and his multiplication plan. She argued with them about the benefits of having family planning, but it was useless. Nobody was willing to hear her.

The discussion became so heated that law enforcement had to intervene to reestablish the order. The officers had to threaten some men with prison for them to leave the missionary alone and allow her to continue talking to the women.

After some weeks, medical teams arrived at Leontino and attended to everyone, teaching them about birth control and familiar planning. The visitors explained to them many crucial questions, examined women, prescribed contraceptives, distributed condoms, and scheduled some surgical procedures.

Some men had changed their minds and were also attended. They were a minority, but their actions gave some hope for Simone.

During that day, Simone met a man who was a missionary

in a neighbor's town. They talked a lot about their experiences, challenges, and everything else. At the end of that day, they committed themselves to keep in touch.

Another time, Simone's church reduced her wage and financial support. She demanded explanations, but there was no concrete answer. Simone suspected the church did not agree with her reforms in Leontino. Months later, her suspicions were confirmed. A close friend called her and explained all that was happening. The church's management was uncomfortable with the changes in the town. Many people in the church thought Simone should only teach and evangelize; she had not been sent to make progressive reforms and alter social order and traditions.

The missionary got sad by these words; she prayed to God asking Him to help her in that situation because she had doubts about her purpose.

She opened her Bible in Matthew, chapter five.

13 "You are the salt of the earth. But if the salt loses its saltiness, how can it be made salty again? It is no longer good for anything, except to be thrown out and trampled underfoot. 14 "You are the light of the world. A town built on a hill cannot be hidden. 15 Neither do people light a lamp and put it under a bowl. Instead they put it on its stand, and it gives light to everyone in the house. 16 In the same way, let your light shine before others, that they may see your good deeds and glorify your Father in heaven.

Simone sighed and said, "Oh Lord, I wanna be salt and light for these people, but it seems that nobody wants it. I'm doing my best, but even the church is limiting me. Lord, help me to continue making a difference and preaching your word."

The missionary was getting tired and discouraged; however, she did not give up or give in. Simone found solid and kind support in that man she kept in touch with. They started dating, and true love rose in their hearts.

Year after year, the classes increased the number of students. After the initial transformations, more people were confident that education could lead them to a better future. The youth of Leontino dreamed of a new life, new standards, and breakthroughs. For the first time in that town, they could see themselves in a lifestyle different from their parents. Boys and girls did not see themselves as poor young parents, farmworkers, and housewives. They began to believe they could reach higher positions, move away from that isolated place, and build a fresh and blessed life.

These young people told their parents about their perspectives, and the reaction was terribly worse than they expected. Virtually all the parents discouraged and rebuked their children. They said these ideas were not for them; all were only illusions sown by Simone, and none of them would achieve it. Even the parents watering their dreams down, they did not believe. Each teenager continued seeking their dreams.

Once again, the people of Leontino argued with Simone because of the dreams of the teenagers. People accused and insulted her with every swear word they knew. They put her on charges of being against family and its values. She was considered a family destroyer, instigating children to leave their parents and live a disorderly life.

This time, law enforcement was reduced in the town, and the mess took an enormous proportion. People vandalized Simone's school and house. They burned notebooks, books, and scholarship materials. At her house, they broke windows, cut off the power and internet, and almost set fire to the house.

Simone was dismayed seeing people's savagery. She cried out for mercy and tried to stop them. But there were too many against her. Some students joined her defense, but they were just a few people against a multitude. The missionary wept bitterly while she saw the destruction. Her fiancé was advised about the chaos and went to Leontino. He drove her out to another place. What happened that day was unbelievable for

Simone; everything seemed a nightmare.

Despite the witch-hunt, Simone returned to Leontino. She walked slowly through the ruins of the school; she looked at the destruction scenario and remembered all she lived there, since the first time she entered that room. All those dreams of the past were burned by ignorance. She was deeply moved, and the tears downed.

So, she went to her house and saw almost the same situation; the only difference was the absence of fire, but the rest was like the school: messed up, destroyed, and everything spread for every side. As soon as her students knew about her visit, they went to the house and helped her to fix what they could.

And to make things worse, days later, she received several bills for all the damage people had done. The unfairness was immeasurable; she was a victim but has been treated as a criminal. Simone knew she was not able to pay all those bills, but she analyzed them carefully to decide which would be paid.

After paying what she could, all of Simone's money ran out. She only had the money for one more meal, and then, she didn't know how she would survive. Simone had lunch in the cheapest place in the town; she was sitting alone in a corner. While she ate, she thought about her life, from the moment she was invited to the mission until now.

God, was it worth it? She thought sadly. *Was this the Lord dreamed for me? I can't understand why so many tragedies came upon me! I tried to do my best since I received the invitation for this mission, but I always got the worst from everybody. They hate me because of all I've done.*

"Simone?" a male voice called her.

She looked and saw a young man; she had never seen him before.

"If you came to charge me, you must give up!" Simone replied, discouraged. "I spent my last cent on lunch."

"I'm so sorry about what happened to you. I didn't come to charge; I came to give you thanks."

"Did you come to give me thanks?" She was surprised.

"That's it, I'm here to give you thanks. You've blessed my life in a way I can't describe," replied soulfully.

Simone observed him attentively, trying to recognize him, but she could not.

"I'm sorry, but I don't remember you. What's your name?"

"Felipe. You never met me before, but your job helped me."

"How?"

"Can I sit down?"

"Yes, you can."

"I'm from another city, and there, I met one of your alumni. We are in the same college. Wesley was the first person who told me about God, Jesus, and salvation. Initially, I mocked him about this and said I would never frequent a church. But when I almost reached rock bottom, I changed my mind."

"What happened? Can you tell me?"

"I was living as a crazy man: parties, alcohol, drugs, and all you can imagine. I supposed I was controlling my life, but the addictions were controlling me. I drank and consumed drugs every day, and my parents got desperate about my situation. Amid this craziness, Wesley was there, speaking about freedom and a fresh life. He said that Jesus could free me from the addictions, and I would be another person. Wesley repeated that was not the end of my story, and all could be different. He was like a broken record; it was annoying; however, his faith gave me the confidence to seek my freedom. I went to rehabilitation, and God gifted me with a fresh life. I'm fighting every day against addiction; it's a tough battle, but I know that I have a true friend who supports me, and I have the Almighty God to hold my hands. I'm not alone anymore. All this was possible because you were his teacher; you taught him scholarly subjects, and he could join the college. And you also taught him about faith, so he could teach me. Indirectly, you are part of my salvation."

Felipe's story deeply moved Simone. She understood that her purpose was bigger than Leontino, and maybe she would not see all the fruits of her work, but God would.

She smiled and said, "Wow! What an overcoming story! I feel honored to be part of it."

"I wanna support your work to continue helping people."

"Thank you, but after the last happenings, I need a lot of resources."

"Don't worry," he smiled, "my parents have all you need, and they'll be very generous."

Hope was born again in Simone's heart. At that moment, she recognized that God was always blessing her work.

My Last Day of Sadness

At night, a man about forty years old was walking on a street in formal wear. He always had a happy expression and greeted everyone he saw on the street.

He entered a bakeshop and bought a water bottle. When he came out, he saw a middle-aged man sitting on the curb. He wore dirty clothes and had a plastic liquor bottle on his side. It was not the first time he saw that scene.

"José!" he said to the man on the curb. "Why are you sitting on the ground?"

"Pastor Henrique," José replied, smiling with a drunken voice, "I'm at ease here. If I want, I can even lie down."

The pastor squatted down and looked at his tired and sad eyes. He said compassionately, "José, I've already said you should care for yourself. You can't stay thrown on the ground or the streets. You deserve a better life."

"Pastor, look at me. I'm a drunken man. Do you really think I deserve something better?"

"For sure, I believe!" he replied confidently, "you're not a drunken man; you're a person in a temporary drunken situation. You're a son of the Most High God! You can overcome this situation and go to a bright future. You deserve everything good

57

in your life."

The man smiled and said, "The pastor says it with so much confidence. I almost believe it."

"You should believe. It's not me saying. It's God saying to you."

For an instant, José thought about living differently. But he looked at the liquor bottle and changed his mind.

"Pastor, your words are so touching. But I suppose this isn't for me. I'm old and disheveled. Look at my appearance: dirty, beard and long hair." He smelled himself and continued, "A little stinking. Would God wanna someone like me?"

"God doesn't love us because of our appearance. He loves us because of our hearts. If you believe and give your life to him, he will welcome you with open arms. Jesus will hug you and walk with you," Henrique said boldly.

José sighed and said doubtfully, "Maybe one day. I think I'm not ready yet."

"Don't delay making a decision. None of us knows the time we've left."

"Don't be a scaremonger. I'm sure I have too much time. If I've reached fifty…" José was confused, "Or I'm forty-nine? Let me see."

José took his billfold from his shirt pocket and caught a

document; he tried to read it but could not. So, he asked Henrique, "Please, tell me my age."

Henrique took the document, analyzed it, and said, "You're forty-nine until today. Tomorrow you'll be fifty!" He said excitedly, "I'm sure it'll be a great day."

"It'll be an ordinary day like all my days!" José replied, discouraged, "It won't take place anything special."

"What about your family and friends?" Henrique asked in surprise.

"Friends? This isn't part of my life! Who do you think wanna be friends with a drunken man?"

"And your family?"

"Pastor, don't you know my story?"

"We've already talked other times, but you didn't tell me about your past."

"If you have time, I can tell you now."

Henrique was going to a service where he would preach; however, he understood he could not leave José that moment.

"Wait for a moment, please."

Henrique got up and called someone; he said he could not preach that day. Thus, he entered the bakeshop and returned with two chairs for him and José.

They sat; José took a deep breath and said sadly, "It's a little hard for me to tell my own story. Formerly, everything was different..."

José remembered how his life used to be. Then, he was younger and well-groomed; he walked on the streets as Henrique did, smiling, happy, and in high spirits.

He entered his home and was greeted by a wonderful woman. She hugged him tightly and kissed him passionately.

"My love!" he said excitedly, "I love you so much!"

"We love you so much!" she replied in the same tone while caressing her womb.

José bent down and said close to her womb, "I already love you, my baby!"

"Do you remember our medical appointment tomorrow?" she asked.

"Of course! I'm anxious to know if we'll have a boy or a girl."

"Me too!"

"As soon as we know, we can prepare their room."

"I have too many ideas!" she exclaimed with enthusiasm.

"I'm sure you don't have better ideas than me. If it's a boy, we'll buy a crib and a bed with a car shape. If it's a girl, it'll be a mermaid shape."

She laughed and said, "Whether they're better, I don't

know, but your ideas are certainly crazier than mine."

"We must do our best for our baby!"

"However, we don't need to do the craziest things. Let's wait for tomorrow, and then we'll decide what to buy."

The couple continued talking about their plans for the baby's room.

The next day, they went to a medical appointment. A female doctor assisted them during the ultrasound. She looked surprised by those images. The couple noticed her reaction and got concerned.

"Doctor," she said apprehensively, "is everything right with my baby?"

"Natália," the doctor replied, "is everything right with your two babies. Congrats, you'll have twins, a boy and a girl."

"Are you serious?" Natália could not believe it.

"Pinch me, I must be dreaming!" José was too excited about that piece of news.

The doctor smiled and said, "I know this is mind-blowing, but you've been blessed with a couple. That's very rare."

"Thanks to God!" José shouted.

Natália's eyes were filled with tears, and she said, "That's amazing!"

José and Natália were impressed by that; they longed for a

baby for so long, and now, they would have two.

The couple left the medical appointment and went to several stores to buy furniture for the twins' room.

Months passed, and the room was ready for Amanda and Miguel. Half of it was pink, and the other half blue. They filled all the space with all types of cute things: letters spelling out the babies' names, wallpapers with whimsical designs, personalized artwork and prints, storage ottoman, baby toys, etc. Both of them put all their love into that work.

On the day of the cesarean, the couple went to the hospital, and there were no complications; everything happened as the doctors planned.

Days after the birth, they were returning home; José was driving, and Natália and the babies were in the back seat. They were happy and excited to start their new life as a family. The car passed through an intersection on the green light and was hit by a red-light runner bus.

José woke up weeks later and knew he was the only survivor of the crash; his wife and babies passed away and had been buried. He sank into a deep state of melancholy and depression; nothing made sense to him.

He entered the babies' room and imagined all his family could have experienced there; however, all was only imagination and fantasy. None of his thoughts would take place.

José attempted to get some relief by drinking a champagne bottle he had saved to celebrate the arrival of the children.

"Pastor, since that day, I always have a bottle next to me."

Henrique was deeply moved by José's story. He felt a mix of feelings: compassion, pity, sadness, empathy, etc. The pastor understood what had led José to alcohol addiction; the losses definitively shook him.

"José, I'm really so sorry for what happened to you. I have no words to comfort you about it."

"Thank you, pastor," José shook his liquor bottle and said, "In some way, I found something to comfort me."

"I suppose…" Henrique forgot what he would say and froze.

José's eyes were attentive to him, waiting for the conclusion. Henrique felt as if someone had interrupted him and whispered something in his ears.

"Pastor? Are you fine?"

Henrique returned to his senses and said, "I'm fine. I had an amazing idea!" he cheerfully said.

"Can you tell me what you thought?"

"Tomorrow!"

"Tomorrow?"

"Yes, can I meet you at home in the morning?"

"I think so," José replied suspiciously, "the pastor started to behave strangely. What happened?"

"If I tell you, I'm sure you won't believe it. I just ask you one thing, please, don't drink anything else from now on," Henrique asked seriously.

"I'll try to be sober, but I can't promise anything."

"You'll get it! I believe that God will give you strength to resist," he said confidently.

"I think I'll get it only because of your boldness."

"Amen! You'll do it!" Henrique stated confidently. "And to guarantee it, I'll take this."

Henrique took the liquor bottle.

José smiled and said, "Does the pastor know if I wanna another one, I can buy it?"

"Yes, I do. But I trust in you; I trust you won't do it."

"The pastor is more confident in me than I am in myself."

"Believe, José, you'll stay sober until tomorrow." Henrique was very confident.

They said goodbye, and Henrique went away thinking about what he would do. He had many ideas and called some people who could help him.

The next morning, Henrique was in front of José's home early. He knocked on the gate and heard a reply, "I'm going!"

José opened the gate and said, "Pastor, are you an early bird? I supposed you would arrive a bit later."

Henrique noticed that he seemed sober and asked to confirm, "Are you sober?"

"Yes. I don't know how I got it. Since our conversation, I didn't feel like drinking anything."

"I said that God would give you strength to resist."

"Maybe," José replied doubtfully.

"Don't doubt. God is helping you."

"Maybe…" José continued, doubting.

"Let's go for a ride. We have too many things to do!" he said with excitement.

"Do we have?" José asked in surprise.

"Yes, we have. Get into my car."

"Wait a minute; I have to lock the door."

"Okay."

José entered his house and came back quickly. They got into the car and went away.

"Where are we going?" José asked.

"Soon, you'll see."

"The pastor is mysterious. What happened?"

"At the end of the day, I'll tell you."

"Each answer you give me makes me more curious."

"Don't worry," Henrique smiled. "I have good plans for your day."

Henrique drove for some minutes and smiled as he saw his destination.

"Here is our first stop!" Henrique announced, parking the car.

José looked around and said, surprised, "Are we at the right place?"

"Yes, we're."

They stopped in front of a barbershop.

"I don't need a new haircut."

"For sure, you need it. Let's go!"

"Alright," he agreed, discouraged.

They entered the place, and the male barber was smiling and waiting close to a chair.

"Welcome, José!" the barber said enthusiastically, "Are you ready for a transformation?"

"And do I have a choice?" he asked Henrique.

"No, you don't." Henrique smiled.

"Please, sit and relax," the barber asked him.

José sat, and the barber pulled a thin string. A curtain covered the mirror.

"Won't I see what you are doing to me?"

"It'll be a surprise!" Henrique replied.

"One more surprise, don't pastor?"

Henrique smiled and replied, "Yes, one more surprise."

The barber started his job. He cut José's hair and shaved him. So, he washed and combed him.

José was in front of the covered mirror; he ran his hands over his head, trying to figure out what he looked like.

"José," Henrique said, "are you ready to see a new man?"

"I don't know if only a haircut and a shave could make me a new man. But I'm anxious to see me."

"Look at the fresh José!" the barber said while opening the curtain.

José looked attentively at the reflected image. He touched his face as he did not believe what he was seeing. José analyzed all the details of that new man.

"My jaw is on the floor! It's unbelievable what you've done," José said.

José felt as if something had borne again within; he could see himself handsome and respectable after so long. He held himself back from crying.

"Thank you very much!" José thanked the barber with all his heart.

The man hugged him and replied, "God sees you as a

masterpiece, a precious stone, and a perfect diamond. Start to see yourself in this way."

"I'll try it."

"You won't try!" Henrique said confidently, "You'll get it."

"Alright, pastor," José said, "I'll get it."

They said goodbye to the barber and continued their ride. José looked at himself in the mirrors almost the whole time. His transformation was incredible and tremendous.

"Pastor, I have to thank you once more! That was amazing."

"Calm down, José." Henrique smiled. "This is just the beginning."

After some minutes, they stopped.

José observed the store and said smiling, "Does the pastor want to rebuild me?"

"Of course, today it'll start a new stage of your life."

This time, it was a clothing store. They entered, and a couple welcomed them.

"Good morning, José!" The woman greeted José joyfully.

"Welcome to our store!" The man said in the same joyful tone.

"Good morning," José replied.

"My friends," Henrique said, "I'm sure that you'll give a new style to José."

"We've prepared our best for him!" The man replied enthusiastically.

"José," Henrique said to him, "you are in good hands, enjoy it."

"Alright."

Henrique said to the couple, "Do you remember what to do?"

"Yes, we do," the woman replied, "our mirrors are covered.

José looked at Henrique and exclaimed in disapproval, "Pastor! Again?"

Henrique smiled and said, "It'll be another surprise."

"Alright."

The couple introduced José to some fashion styles, and he tried some of them. After choosing what he would use, he came back to Henrique.

The pastor looked at him and said confidently, "This is the man who God created you to be! Let's see a blessed and strong man?"

José smiled and said, "It's funny the way you talk about me. Let's see myself in the mirror."

The mirror was uncovered, and José observed himself from top to bottom. He noticed the cleanness and beauty of those new clothes and shoes.

He was transported to the past when he and Natália went to buy clothes. All that excitement and desire to be well-dressed was born again in his heart.

"I'm floored!" José was stunned. "You brought me back to one of the happiest moments of my life."

The man hugged him and said confidently, "God gives us happy moments every day. Accept what God can do in your life."

"Thank you for your words." José smiled and said, "Pastor, if you continue in this rhythm, I'll trust in all these words."

"You can believe," Henrique replied, "this is the truth about you."

"I don't know yet."

"But soon, you'll be assured! Let's continue our ride?"

"Let's go!"

José said goodbye to the couple with many thankful words; he and Henrique continued on their journey.

It was about midday, and Henrique stopped in front of a restaurant.

"I think this place is familiar," José said.

"Have you ever eaten here?"

"I think so," he replied doubtfully.

"When?"

"I don't remember."

"Let's have lunch; I'm sure you'll remember."

They entered that place, and the chef was waiting for them. He smiled and said, "Welcome to my restaurant, José."

José looked attentively at that middle-aged man like he recognized him. He searched deep into his mind and remembered.

"Francis?"

"I knew you'd recognize and remember me!" Francis said with excitement.

José looked around, noticing all the objects in that place. That vision brought him back to his best moments, where he and his wife frequented the restaurant. That was their favorite place.

"Things are a little different," José said, "but I remember most of them," he said nostalgically.

He walked through the room and touched the chairs, tables, objects, etc.

"Pastor," José said, "Why are you doing this? Why are you trying to bring me back to my past?"

Henrique got close to him and gently replied, "I'm not trying to bring you back to your past. I'm trying to bring happiness to your life."

"How could I be happy again? I lost everything I've loved."

"But you didn't lose your life. Your beloved ones passed away, but you continue here. Did you already think what your wife would say if she saw you like yesterday? What she'd say seeing her husband drunken, dirty, and thrown on the ground? I'm sure that she'd wish the best for you. She'd wish to see you sober, healthy, handsome, and well-nourished. I'm trying to remember who you really are."

Who am I? José thought. *Could I be that respectable man again? Or am I an old and drunken man?*

José saw some drink bottles on a shelf and a mirror behind them. He could almost feel the taste of the drinks, so he looked at his reflection. José saw half of his face in his new appearance and the other half he was like the previous day.

"My eternal love," he said crying, "for you, I wanna my best version again."

José walked towards Henrique and hugged him tightly while saying, "Pastor, what I'm feeling now is beyond what I can express with words. I supposed I'd never feel it again. But thanks to you, I'm feeling alive again. Thank you so much!"

José released all his tears, and Henrique said gently, "You're welcome, but I'm only a servant of God. You must give thanks to him. He's freeing you from your past sufferings and showing a fresh start."

"I wanna be free and have a fresh start," José replied, drying his tears. "What do I have to do?"

"Let's sit, and I'm gonna tell you."

They sat and had lunch while Henrique was explaining to José some steps he could take, like walking in God's path, counseling, medical and psychological support, rehabilitation, etc. The pastor could see that José was extremely interested in all these things. José seemed to be ready to start a new and blessed life.

After lunch, José felt mild abdominal pains and said smiling, "I think I ate too much, my belly isn't getting used to this amount of food."

"From now on, you'll re-educate your body for a new phase."

"For sure! The beginning is today!" José stated confidently.

"Now, let's go to our next-to-last appointment!"

"Next-to-last? Do I still have two more appointments?"

"Yes, you do."

They got into the car and went to their next destination. Henrique parked, and José said, "Don't you think I'm too old for this?"

Henrique smiled and replied, "Nobody is too old for fun.

You deserve it. When was the last time you had fun?"

"I don't remember."

"Let's have fun!" Henrique stated confidently.

They spent the whole afternoon at an amusement park. José has played and enjoyed it like he was a child. They played on roller coaster, Ferris wheel, bumper cars, and carousel; they also played games and won prizes galore.

Happiness and excitement filled José's mind and body; while he was in the park, he did not remember any sadness in his life. It was like he had been born again and had started a new life that day; José had been taken from the darkness of anguish and led to the light of joyfulness.

They were leaving the park, and José noticed an awe-inspiring sunset; he delighted himself with the colors' beauty and nuances. The sky had many stunning tones, mixing blue, yellow, orange, and red. The sun had touched the horizon, and they could see only a half of it.

José took a deep breath and said with all his heart, "God, thank you for this day, thank you for this magnificent vision, thank you for everything the Lord made for me today."

Glory to God! Henrique thought. *The Lord has healed his broken heart and spirit. He's a new man.*

"Pastor, let's go to my last appointment?" José said with

excitement.

"That's the spirit!" Henrique replied in the same excited manner.

They came back to their neighborhood. Henrique returned to the church; the lights were turned off, and the place was closed.

"Pastor, why are we here?" José asked in surprise.

"I forgot a thing inside there. Can you help me to pick it up and put it in my car?"

"Yes, I can."

Henrique opened the door, and as soon as they entered, all the lights were turned on; there was a huge happy birthday banner and too many people. And everyone they had met during the day was there as well.

They sang in one voice, "Happy birthday to you! Happy birthday to you! Happy birthday dear José! We and God love you! May your dreams all come true!"

José did not resist, and the tears came.

"This is the best day ever!" he said, deeply touched, "I can't believe I'm living this."

While people were still singing, someone got close to him, pushing a desk with a birthday cake with a sparkling candle.

José's tears increased, and he hugged Henrique; he tried to

give him thanks, but the emotion did not allow him to say anything.

Henrique understood what he wanted to say and replied, "You deserve it; you're precious; God loves you."

José contained his tears and was greeted and blessed by everyone. All the people said words of encouragement to him.

At one point, Henrique took a microphone and said, "José, please, say some words."

José was a bit nervous, but he took the microphone.

"The first thing I have to say is thank you very much! I'd spend the whole night thanking everyone here. I'd never imagined I'd experience what I experienced today. Yesterday, at this very hour, I was dirty and thrown on the ground. And now, I'm clean and standing. All this was possible only because of one man." José looked at Henrique and continued, "The pastor Henrique believed in me even when I didn't believe. He said I wasn't a drunken man and could have a better life. And today, I'm living this better life. Once more, thank you, pastor."

People applauded José's speech, and he delivered the microphone to Henrique.

"Thank you for your words, José. But I must confess that what happened today wasn't only because of me. All the people here share the responsibility. Since we talked yesterday, I started calling and sending messages to everyone. I've asked everyone I know for help, and all of them could provide something to make your day special. José, at the beginning of this day, you've asked me what happened to be doing this. Do you remember?"

José shook his head positively.

"Yesterday, when we're talking, I'd rebuke you because you had said you found comfort in the liquor. But at that very time, I heard the wonderful voice of the Holy Spirit saying to me, 'Show him love with actions, don't just criticize.' This advice made me think about my behavior, and I decided to give you the best birthday you ever had. I suppose I got it."

"Of course! You've got it!" José agreed.

"Now, I must ask you one thing. Do you wanna give your life to Jesus? Do you wanna a new life with God?"

José made a thoughtful expression, generating suspense in everyone. He took the microphone and said, "If giving my life to Jesus means having a lot of people caring about me and showing their love, my answer is yes!" he said assuredly, "I wanna be part of God's family! I wanna be with Jesus all my days!"

People shouted many words of praise.

"Glory to God!"

"Hallelujah!"

"God is awesome!"

"José," Henrique said, "close your eyes and repeat a prayer with me."

José did it and prayed with all his heart, "Lord Jesus, I repent of my sins and surrender my life. Wash me clean. I believe that Jesus Christ is the Son of God. That he died on the cross for my sins and rose again on the third day for my victory. I believe that in my heart and confess with my mouth, that Jesus is my Savior and Lord. I receive eternal life, in Jesus' name. Amen."

Everyone applauded and shouted more words of praise.

José continued celebrating his birthday and his new beginning. At one point, he felt abdominal pains again, but this time it was severe. José was sitting and passed his hand over his belly, trying to massage it.

Henrique got close, noticed his painful expression, and asked, "José, are you okay?"

"Pastor..." he could hardly reply, "something is wrong with me. I feel a strong pain in my abdomen."

José coughed and put his hand in his mouth; he felt a strange taste and looked at the palm of his hand.

"Pastor," José said in fear, "I need help."

He showed his hand to Henrique, and there was blood on it.

"Oh, my God!" Henrique was amazed. "Let's go to the hospital."

Henrique took José's arm to help him get up. He could only take two steps and fell on the floor, contorting in pain.

"I can't continue!" he shouted.

Some men got close and carried José to Henrique's car. He drove as fast as he could to the hospital. José continued coughing and expelling blood; his shirt got splashed in red.

They reached the hospital, and José was rushed to the emergency room. Henrique stayed in the waiting room, praying all the time.

After some hours, he looked at his watch and saw it was a little after midnight.

A female doctor arrived and said, "Who is with José?"

"I'm with him!" He said while getting up. "How is he?"

"I'm sorry," she replied in sadness, "we did our best, but he passed away."

The doctor's words reverberated in his mind: "He passed away." It was impossible. Just hours ago, José had beamed like a man born anew, lit by God's blessing and surrounded by love. He had laughed, prayed, and sang with joy, not pain.

"Oh, God! It's hard to believe. Yesterday was so special. What happened to him?"

"He had several tumors in his liver. I don't know how he could live like that. Do you know if he was undergoing treatment?"

"I suppose he did not even know about the tumors."

"How is this possible?" The doctor asked, amazed. "His condition was critical; it most probably he had some symptoms."

"His life was a bit complicated," Henrique said sadly, "he fought against addiction and loneliness."

"These are two difficult things to deal with and can consume anyone."

They continued talking a little more, so the doctor went away.

Henrique sat down and downed his head; he prayed sadly, "Lord God, it's hard to understand why this happened. José was so happy yesterday; he had given his life to you, Lord. And now, I'm sure that he is on your side. The Lord gave him a new life, the eternal life. He'll never feel any pain or sadness again; he'll never suffer for anything. I'm sure all happened according to the Lord's will and plan. And your plans are perfect."

The next day, the church hosted a solemn funeral ceremony. Everyone who was at the party was there. Nobody believed that really had happened. It seemed illogical and incomprehensible. José had his best and last day at once.

Henrique climbed onto the pulpit and said sadly, "Dear brothers and sisters, today is a day of weeping and sadness for us. However, it's a day of joy and happiness in Heaven. God received a beloved son in his arms. This son lived as the prodigal son, apart from God's path, but he could find it again. I asked God why he did this. And through his word, God answered me. Psalms thirty-four, verse twenty-two, says: 'The Lord will rescue his servants; no one who takes refuge in him will be condemned.' I faithfully believe that God rescued José. God put a definitive end to his sad story and took him to eternal happiness. This is the same hope for all of us who believe in God. May José's last day can be an example for everyone; a sample of what God can do through his servants and for his servants. We provided him a remarkable day, marked the difference in his life, and brought light into darkness; we've accomplished our mission as Christians."

Henrique continued with more encouraging words. Then, the funeral procession went to the graveyard. José was buried on the side of his family.

After these happenings, Henrique's church became more engaged in supporting the neighborhood. They did their best to help everyone with their needs, no matter their need.

Because of its actions, the church became a reference in the city and was highly appreciated by all people.

Is God Here?

"This is the will of God for his people!" A man cried out dramatically in the pulpit of a Protestant church.

All the people applauded his speech, and many cried words of praise. And those were not the usual screams heard in the churches; they were extremely dramatic and almost theatrical.

Most of the people shouted hysterically, and besides the shouts, they moved uncontrollably, trembled, fell to the floor, and spun with open arms. That service was a mess; nobody could understand what was taking place. And the more people became confused, the more the man in the pulpit screamed dramatically.

Amid all this peculiar service, a woman was sitting on a padded chair, observing everything. This young woman observed and was confused.

God, is this right? She thought. *Is this a service to God? What's happening here?*

She lowered her head, sighed, and prayed with all her heart, "Lord, is there something wrong with me? Why can't I feel and act like everyone?"

Fernanda had many doubts about her faith and God's action in her life. She felt like a fish out of water, and this was not the first time she felt like that; she had a long-term inner conflict.

Years ago, Fernanda had been introduced to Protestantism. She grew up in a Catholic family, and all she knew about religion came from her early years, childhood, and adolescence.

She participated in several Catholic sacraments, such as Baptism, Eucharist, and Confirmation. Fernanda tried to keep herself faithful until her adolescence. At this moment, she was the only one in her house concerned about religion; her parents had abandoned their faith. However, they never admitted it. They continued saying to everyone they were Catholic, continued with the rosary in the rearview mirror, and a Holy Bible opened in Psalm twenty-three over a piece of furniture in the living room.

Fernanda tried to encourage them to go to church, but they always refused, saying, "The most important thing is my faith. We don't need to go to a place to pray. God is everywhere." Little by little, their excuses discouraged her, and she did not insist anymore.

After Fernanda started her first job, she could not reconcile her agenda. She often worked during Mass time or was too tired to go there. Gradually, Fernanda moved away from the Catholic Church.

Even with the distancing, she did not abandon her faith; she continued believing and praying to God. She read the Bible and did her best to maintain the Christian faith.

About twenty and some, Fernanda dated a Protestant young man. He introduced her to the faith again. She started to frequent his church and learned new things about God, Jesus Christ, the Holy Spirit, etc.

After several months, she decided to baptize and start a new faith life. At that moment, Fernanda felt she needed to be close to God again; she did not want to follow alone in her path.

Unfortunately, her dating did not endure, and she moved away from that community. Again, Fernanda continued faithful to God, praying, reading the Bible, obeying God's commandments and principles, and doing her best as a Christian.

She often visited some churches, big, small, famous, and unknown, but she did not become a member of any of them.

Therefore, not even Fernanda knew what she was seeking, then, she could not decide.

After a long workday, Fernanda was walking in a street close to her house and heard a Christian song playing. This one was a little different from what she was used to hearing. It was exciting music, and everyone in the church seemed to be singing.

"It seems interesting," she said.

Fernanda followed the song and found out where the church was. It was not a classical building; it was a big metal gate with a ramp inside to access the room.

She read the name on the sign, smiled, and said, "Intercontinental Ministry Time of Fruitfulness. It's a very peculiar name."

She also read the services' hours and looked at her phone's clock.

"I suppose the service is almost over. I'll visit this place another day."

Fernanda went home thinking about the church and its service. Days later, she visited it on a Sunday, its main service.

She was welcomed by a gentle and smiling couple.

"Good evening!" They greeted her warmly.

Fernanda smiled and replied, "Good evening."

The woman gave him a tight hug and said, "Welcome to our church!" The woman continued with the same tone. "We're glad to have you here."

"Thank you," Fernanda replied.

The man greeted her with a handshake and said excitedly, "I'm sure you'll have an amazing and blessed moment."

"Amen!" She responded like them because she was

captivated by their energy.

"Is it your first time here?" The woman asked.

"Yes."

"I'm gonna show you everything."

"Thank you."

Fernanda was impressed by her disposition; it was the first time she had this type of treatment.

The woman accompanied Fernanda through the church; it was an ordinary rectangular building with white walls and rows of padded chairs. The altar was an elevated rectangle with three steps and a transparent glass pulpit; the musicians and their instruments were also there; there was ample space between the altar and the first row of chairs.

Fernanda was led to a middle-aged couple in formal clothes, and the receptionist said with excitement, "These are our blessed apostles, Paulo e Paula. They founded this congregation."

Apostles? Fernanda thought in surprise. *Shouldn't they be pastors?*

"Welcome to our blessed family!" Paulo and Paula said with excitement.

"Thank you," Fernanda replied.

"This church is your house. Make yourself at home!" Paulo

continued.

"We have a special place for you," Paula said.

They led Fernanda to a chair in the first row, and she got embarrassed for being put in such a high position.

"Don't care about me; I can sit anywhere!"

"You're a very special visitor! You deserve it!" Paula said.

"Alright."

She sat down, and the apostles and the receptionist returned to their positions.

After some minutes, the service started like the others she had gone to. Someone has read a biblical text and prayed. So, the musicians started. All the songs were lively. During each song, two or three girls were dancing close to the altar. They wore white long-sleeved shirts and trousers made of satin and a pretty colored skirt. They danced freely according to the music beat and lyrics.

Fernanda enjoyed the moment of praise; she sang and praised God with all her heart.

The songs finished, and the apostle Paulo went up to the pulpit; he greeted people excitedly, "The grace of God be with you all!"

"Amen!" they replied.

"Today, we have special people among us, the visitors.

Please, stand up, Fernanda, Leonardo, Tamires, Ricardo, and Luana."

Fernanda and the other visitors stood up.

"What do we say to them?" asked the apostle.

All people replied excitedly, "You're welcome in our church and our hearts. We are glad about your visit, and God is still more pleased. We love you!"

So, they applauded, and the entire church went to greet them with hugs and handshakes.

They're so warm-hearted. Fernanda thought.

The meeting continued with the sermon; Paulo talked about commitment to God and his work. He highlighted the importance of working for God and his kingdom.

After finishing his sermon, Paulo called people who wanted to renew their commitment to God to go close to the altar. Many people went there, and he prayed for them.

The sermon was so impactful. Fernanda thought.

Paulo called Paula, and she finished that ceremony with blessing words for the people.

The receptionist got close to Fernanda and delivered her a card with information about the church services schedule, apostles' and assistants' phone numbers, and other information.

"If you need anything, you can call us," the woman said

gently.

"You're so attentive," Fernanda replied, enchanted.

"This is our mission as Christians, supporting each other," the woman replied confidently.

These words touched Fernanda's heart. Even being her first time there, she felt embraced by that church and part of that community. This feeling made her decide to visit them again.

Fernanda was welcomed like the first time and sat in the first row once more. This time, things ran out of the script. While the song was playing, Paulo went to the pulpit and started to speak unintelligible words, igniting a sparkle of euphoria in the church. Several people started speaking unintelligible words. And many of them were almost screaming; it initiated a little mess in the ambiance.

This is strange. Fernanda thought. *I've already heard that the Holy Spirit manifests himself in many ways, but everything must be done in a fitting and orderly way.*

The mess continued a little more. People fell backward to the floor, and the assistants supported their falls, so they did not fall violently and covered them with linen sheets.

It was the first time Fernanda saw such a spectacle; she believed everything was happening because of the Holy Spirit's presence.

Fernanda had watched the same spectacle at every meeting and got used to it; she had convinced herself the Holy Spirit could act in many ways; this was enough for her.

At one service, Fernanda went close to the altar after Paulo's calling, hoping she would be touched by the Holy Spirit, speak unintelligible words, and fall to the floor. However, this time, nothing happened.

I suppose this isn't the right moment for me. She thought.

Fernanda always repeated this action, and nothing happened. She felt she was not worthy of receiving the same gift as everyone else. However, she did not give up on getting it.

She became an official church member and had close contact with the apostles and their family. All the members revered them like God's anointed ones; nobody could disagree with their ideas or commands. People treated them like vice gods, providing everything they needed in church and their personal lives. This behavior seemed odd to Fernanda, but she acted like everyone because she respected the apostles as spiritual authorities.

Months later, the city where Fernanda lived was experiencing a critical epidemic of dengue fever; many church members were affected. In all services, they prayed to God and warned about what people could do to prevent the disease.

The epidemic intensified, and the church continued its efforts to support the members. Fernanda considered one of these efforts controversial.

At a service, Paulo and Paula were in the pulpit, and he said confidently, "Brothers and sisters, God provided a solution for this terrible dengue epidemic."

Some people shouted words of praise.

"Hallelujah!"

"Glory to God!"

Paulo continued enthusiastically, "The assistants will give you a water bottle. But this isn't usual water. This water was anointed. My wife and I went to the mountain and prayed fervently to God, and he showed that we should do this. We anointed and consecrated the water with pure olive oil from Israel, and now, it's the healing water. Take a bottle and see the miracle in your home."

People shouted more words of praise.

Oh, God! Fernanda thought in disbelief. *What's this? Anointed and consecrated water? Are we in a Roman Catholic Church?*

Fernanda doubted that the proposal was correct and according to God's guidance.

But people reveled in it; there was another spectacle of

unintelligible words and people falling to the floor. The more the mess grew, the more the apostles encouraged people to allow the Holy Spirit to act.

The whole picture of that service was unpleasant to Fernanda; she could not feel nor see God's presence there. All seemed to be directed by the apostles, and people acted as if they were in a trance.

That was the first time that Fernanda was upset about the church; however, it was not the only one.

In another service, there was an invited male musician who played saxophone. He played magnificently, touching all people's hearts with his notes. On this day, there were a lot of visitors to the church.

After his sermon, Paulo said, "I invite all people who want to receive something new from God to come close to the altar."

Virtually the entire church got close. The assistants moved the chairs to free up more space for everyone.

"Now, close your eyes," Paulo said, "our brother will play a blessed song on his saxophone, and I'll pray for the supernatural to come upon us tonight."

The man played, and Paulo prayed. People reacted instantaneously, shouting unintelligible words and falling to the floor.

At one point, the musician came down from the altar and played in front of each person; he did it until they fell.

Fernanda observed that scene with amazement and thought, *I can't believe what I'm seeing! He's playing like a snake charmer. His saxophone is charming the people and makes them react. For sure, this is not the Holy Spirit.*

Once again, the meeting turned into a disorder. Those who saw it would think anything except a Christian ceremony could happen there.

God, is this right? She thought. *Is this a service to God? What's happening here?*

Fernanda prayed and reflected on what was taking place. One more time, she doubted the Holy Spirit's action in that place.

Fernanda arrived home and searched on the internet about Holy Spirit manifestations, speaking unintelligible words, and people falling. She found tons of information, people saying that all were signs of God's presence. And others said that all were only human inventions to make a circus instead of a service. She got confused by multiple answers; however, she was inclined to believe that God was far from these events.

She knelt and prayed with all her heart, "Lord, I don't know what to think about the church." She sighed. "They sing, pray, praise, and preach. And all seems to be real and according to your word. But lately, I'm not assured about your presence in all they do. Many things seem only staging and not reality. I can't continue going to a place where I doubt everything. Lord, have mercy on me and show me the truth."

She continued looking online and prayed a little more; Fernanda tried to understand what she was experiencing in the church.

The end of the year was close, and the church had services focused on this subject. The apostles spoke about changes and new opportunities in the coming year. Their words made sense to everyone because they made them reflect on what they could do differently for their dreams to come true. Paulo and Paula encouraged all the people to strengthen their faith, work hard, and never lose hope.

After each sermon, Fernanda thought, *This is the type of message we need to hear. We need to remember where our hope lies, in God.*

In the next-to-last service of the year, Paula said dramatically, "People blessed by the Lord. God showed me and my husband a new purpose for the next year, a victorious purpose."

People applauded and shouted words of praise.

The last time I heard something like that, people received a bottle of Holy water. What will come now? Fernanda thought.

"God showed us that his people must be bold and believe in his promises of blessings," Paula continued in the same dramatic tone, "God's people must sacrifice and trust in him."

I know what will take place... Fernanda thought discouraged.

"The next year is twenty-twenty-four, and this year will be special. A year full of blessings, breakthroughs, dreams coming true, and all good things you've never imagined."

All the people listened attentively like they were hearing Jesus Christ.

Fernanda could not stop thinking, *Yes, the coming year can be all this and still more. It only depends on God's blessing and our hard work.*

"For all these good things to take place, there is a price; I mean, there is a key."

She can't even disguise her intentions.

"The key is a financial challenge of two thousand twenty-four reais."

Is she crazy? Most people here earn only a little more than a minimum wage, and she's asking for one and a half.

Everyone thought apprehensive about the value, and Paula

noticed their preoccupations.

"Nobody here needs to worry about this money," Paula tried to convince people. "It'll be an investment in God's Kingdom. You'll unlock all blessings in the Realm of Heaven. Remember the word of the Lord: 'Whoever sows sparingly will also reap sparingly, and whoever sows generously will also reap generously.'"

But you forget the continuation of the text: 'Each of you should give what you have decided in your heart to give, not reluctantly or under compulsion, for God loves a cheerful giver.' In this case, people are under pressure and almost being extorted to give.

"Those who dare to believe and sacrifice to God come to the altar."

Only a few people went there, and Paulo said confidently, "I know that it is hard to accept such a challenge, but it's necessary to receive God's blessings. To make it easy for everyone, I have a card machine. You can offer with your credit card and split it into three interest-free installments. I'm doing this so you don't lose your future because of a pocket change."

More people went to the altar after Paulo's explanations.

What? Is he encouraging people to get into debt? This is too much for me!

The proposal of Paulo was unbelievable, unacceptable, astounding, and out of reality. Fernanda had never imagined she would hear such absurdity in her Christian life. She lowered her head and stopped listening to them; her ears were closed for the rest of the service. She only heard some noise instead of the words of the apostles.

Fernanda's heart was filled with doubts about God's action in that church. And besides that, she questioned herself, *Why does the Lord allow such a thing? Why do people deceive others like that?*

Days later, the New Year's service took place, and Fernanda participated because she had some responsibilities.

That night was like all the others Fernanda went to: songs, a sermon, screams of unintelligible words, people falling to the floor, spinning with open arms, etc. Fernanda observed everything attentively.

After some minutes of observation, she thought, *I had doubts if God was here, but after today, I'm sure that God is not here.*

It was almost midnight, and Paulo said, "Get up, blessed people!"

All the people who had fallen to the floor got up almost instantaneously.

He continued, "The New Year is so close, and this is a time of change. It's the moment to start new things in this church. One of them will start right now."

The lights were turned off, and a loud bugle music started.

"The presence of God is among us!" Paulo shouted.

The lights turned on, and some assistants entered the room wearing Jewish priestly robes and carrying a replica of the Ark of the Covenant. They made the whole thing as described in the Old Testament.

Are we Jews or Christians? Fernanda thought. *What will be next? Does the golden lampstand? Or an altar to sacrifice animals?*

She was disturbed about that mixing of beliefs.

The assistants put the ark over a table on the altar, and Paulo said, "Whenever you want to receive more from God, you can touch the Holy Ark, and God will come upon you. I want to see a queue of people thirsty to receive something from God."

People quickly formed a queue. All of them were anxious to touch the ark and be blessed.

Fernanda got up and stared at the ark. She wished to go to the altar and expose the apostles' sin; they were leading people into idolatry. The power was in that object instead of the God who created all the things. Her desire evaporated when she noticed people's faces; they acted like hungry vultures when they find a carcass.

Fernanda just went away under reproachful looks. She arrived home, knelt, and prayed with tears downing, "Why does the Lord allow this kind of spectacle? Why do people deceive other people in this way? Does the Lord not punish sinners?"

She was very disappointed about what was taking place in that church. For her, everything was wrong, and God was not doing anything to stop that blasphemy.

Days later, people from the church called and sought Fernanda, but she refused to answer them. She was upset and did not want to talk to anyone about church or religious topics. It was like she had shut her heart for these questions. She had given up frequenting any church; her mind said that all churches would be far from God, and none could help her.

Fernanda's religious disillusion affected her deeply; she not only stopped going to church. She reduced her prayers and biblical reading. What was an essential part of her life has become something of less importance.

Sometimes, she passed near some church and wished to be part of a community again; however, her previous experience watered her dreams down.

I bet this church is full of mistakes. All of them have. She often thought.

These negative feelings were rooted in Fernanda's heart in a way that she did not remember God anymore; her spiritual life was dead and buried.

Months later, Fernanda was relaxed on the sofa of her house, watching funny videos on YouTube. Suddenly, a video about religion started.

A middle-aged man said, seriously, "God's people, I'm here today to tell you my testimony of faith. I was a member of a church and saw many odd things, like the mess in the service, people falling to the floor, screaming unintelligible words, object's adoration, and other things that I disagreed with and didn't seem appropriate for a Christian church."

He is like me. Fernanda thought.

"During my time in this church, I wondered if something was wrong with me. I've asked God why I couldn't feel and act like everyone. These doubts were consuming me."

His story is getting interesting.

"And, like everyone, I looked online for explanations for what I was experiencing in the church. If you already did this, you know the answers generate more questions." He smiled. "Then, what can we do? Leave the church? Leave God's presence? Become an Atheist?"

I think I'm almost turning into an Atheist.

"No! We need to study God's word and ask him for the answers. I know this seems hard and unbelievable, but if you ask him wholeheartedly, he will answer you. God will show you the truth. I'm sorry to disappoint you, but it's improbable that God will give you a vision from Heaven with angels or a dream with Jesus talking to you. It's most probably that he uses a Bible and someone to talk to you. At this point, you must be open to the voice of God."

This is the hardest part of the faith. Fernanda thought discouraged.

"After much searching, I decided to dedicate myself to studying the word of God. I've set a time for study each day. Before studying, I prayed and cried out for God's help. I begged him to open my mind and talk to me; this was the first step. Then, I researched everything I had doubts about. I didn't search if something was right or wrong; I searched about the subject. For example, I've searched about people falling to the floor during the services. I found biblical quotations agreeing and disagreeing."

How to break this impasse?

"To decide if this practice was wrong or right, I had to read the entire biblical text, not only the verses. When I did it, I got the answer. A complete reading shows you the whole picture of biblical happenings, and you can conclude by yourself if something is right or not. It's a hard job because you need to read many texts several times, take notes, study what you've read, and pray incessantly. Only then, you'll have the answer to your question.

"For the first question, people falling to the floor, I concluded that there is no biblical support for this practice. The situations in the Bible where people fell were so different from what we see today. The first difference is the position; in the Bible, people fell face to the floor, that is, they've prostrated in reverence and were conscious about what was happening. None of them were in a trance.

"Let's read some examples that support this conclusion. Genesis nineteen, verses one and two, 'The two angels arrived at Sodom in the evening, and Lot was sitting in the gateway of the city. When he saw them, he got up to meet them and bowed down with his face to the ground. "My lords," he said, "please turn aside to your servant's house. You can wash your feet and spend the night and then go on your way early in the morning."'

"First Kings eighteen, verses thirty-eight and thirty-nine, 'Then the fire of the Lord fell and burned up the sacrifice, the wood, the stones and the soil, and also licked up the water in the trench. When all the people saw this, they fell prostrate and cried, "The Lord—he is God! The Lord—he is God!"'

"Ezekiel chapter one, from verse twenty-six until chapter two, verse two, 'Above the vault over their heads was what looked like a throne of lapis lazuli, and high above on the throne was a figure like that of a man. I saw that from what appeared to be his waist up he looked like glowing metal, as if full of fire, and that from there down he looked like fire; and brilliant light surrounded him. Like the appearance of a rainbow in the clouds on a rainy day, so was the radiance around him. This was the appearance of the likeness of the glory of the Lord. When I saw it, I fell facedown, and I heard the voice of one speaking. He said to me, "Son of man, stand up on your feet and I will speak to you." As he spoke, the Spirit came into me and raised me to my feet, and I heard him speaking to me.'

"You noticed that all people fell voluntarily, showing reverence for God and his envoys. In the vision of Ezekiel, the angel told him to stand up. We can conclude that when God acts, people are in their perfect senses and express their fear before his presence. I ask you, what happens in some churches does show any reverence or fear of God?"

No, they turned the church into a circus.

"My next point: speaking unintelligible words. This is a

controversial subject throughout Christian history. Its origin is related in Acts, chapter two, verses one to thirteen, 'When the day of Pentecost came, they were all together in one place. Suddenly a sound like the blowing of a violent wind came from heaven and filled the whole house where they were sitting. They saw what seemed to be tongues of fire that separated and came to rest on each of them. All of them were filled with the Holy Spirit and began to speak in other tongues as the Spirit enabled them. Now there were staying in Jerusalem God-fearing Jews from every nation under heaven. When they heard this sound, a crowd came together in bewilderment, because each one heard their own language being spoken. Utterly amazed, they asked: "Aren't all these who are speaking Galileans? Then how is it that each of us hears them in our native language? Parthians, Medes and Elamites; residents of Mesopotamia, Judea and Cappadocia, Pontus and Asia, Phrygia and Pamphylia, Egypt and the parts of Libya near Cyrene; visitors from Rome (both Jews and converts to Judaism); Cretans and Arabs —we hear them declaring the wonders of God in our own tongues!" Amazed and perplexed, they asked one another, "What does this mean?" Some, however, made fun of them and said, "They have had too much wine."'

Reading this text, it becomes easy to understand.

"I suppose you noticed the text is very clear. The apostles began to speak in other tongues, foreign languages, directed by the Holy Spirit. There weren't unintelligible words; each foreigner could understand in their own language.

"There is a complete explanation about speaking in tongues in First Corinthians, chapter fourteen. From verses one to five, Paul says the gift of prophecy is superior to speaking in tongues and also talks about the need for an interpreter, 'Follow the way of love and eagerly desire gifts of the Spirit, especially prophecy. For anyone who speaks in a tongue does not speak to people but to God. Indeed, no one understands them; they utter mysteries by the Spirit. But the one who prophesies speaks to people for their strengthening, encouraging and comfort. Anyone who speaks in a tongue edifies themselves, but the one who prophesies edifies the church. I would like every one of you to speak in tongues, but I would rather have you prophesy. The one who prophesies is greater than the one who speaks in tongues, unless someone interprets, so that the church may be edified.'

"In verses six to twelve, he says that all kinds of sounds, tongues or musical instruments, have some meaning. And without knowing the meaning, nobody can agree with what is said. 'Now, brothers and sisters, if I come to you and speak in tongues, what good will I be to you, unless I bring you some revelation or knowledge or prophecy or word of instruction? Even in the case of lifeless things that make sounds, such as the pipe or harp, how will anyone know what tune is being played unless there is a distinction in the notes? Again, if the trumpet does not sound a clear call, who will get ready for battle? So it is with you. Unless you speak intelligible words with your tongue, how will anyone know what you are saying? You will just be speaking into the air. Undoubtedly there are all sorts of languages in the world, yet none of them is without meaning. If then I do not grasp the meaning of what someone is saying, I am a foreigner to the speaker, and the speaker is a foreigner to me. So it is with you. Since you are eager for gifts of the Spirit, try to excel in those that build up the church.'

"In verses thirteen to seventeen, Paul says the one who prays in a tongue must pray for the interpretation so that people can understand his words. 'For this reason the one who speaks in a tongue should pray that they may interpret what they say. For if I pray in a tongue, my spirit prays, but my mind is unfruitful. So what shall I do? I will pray with my spirit, but I will also pray with my understanding; I will sing with my spirit, but I will also sing with my understanding. Otherwise when you are praising God in the Spirit, how can someone else, who is now put in the position of an inquirer, say "Amen" to your thanksgiving, since they do not know what you are saying? You are giving thanks well enough, but no one else is edified.'

"In verses eighteen and nineteen, Paul states he speaks many tongues, but it's better to speak intelligible words. 'I thank God that I speak in tongues more than all of you. But in the church I would rather speak five intelligible words to instruct others than ten thousand words in a tongue.'

"In verses twenty to twenty-five, the apostle says that many people speaking in tongues at once can be misunderstood by unbelievers, and those may be converted through prophecy. 'Brothers and sisters, stop thinking like children. In regard to evil be infants, but in your thinking be adults. In the Law it is written: "With other tongues and through the lips of foreigners I will speak to this people, but even then they will not listen to me, says the Lord. Tongues, then, are a sign, not for believers but for unbelievers; prophecy, however, is not for unbelievers but for believers. So if the whole church comes together and everyone speaks in tongues, and inquirers or unbelievers come in, will they not say that you are out of your mind? But if an unbeliever or an inquirer comes in while everyone is prophesying, they are convicted of sin and are brought under judgment by all, as the secrets of their hearts are laid bare. So they will fall down and worship God, exclaiming, "God is really among you!"'

The mess in the church misunderstands even the believers.

"Finishing his explanations, from verses twenty-six to thirty-three, Paul advises people to have order in the church during the meetings. 'What then shall we say, brothers and sisters? When you come together, each of you has a hymn, or a word of instruction, a revelation, a tongue or an interpretation. Everything must be done so that the church may be built up. If anyone speaks in a tongue, two—or at the most three—should speak, one at a time, and someone must interpret. If there is no interpreter, the speaker should keep quiet in the church and speak to himself and to God. Two or three prophets should speak, and the others should weigh carefully what is said. And if a revelation comes to someone who is sitting down, the first speaker should stop. For you can all prophesy in turn so that everyone may be instructed and encouraged. The spirits of prophets are subject to the control of prophets. For God is not a God of disorder but of peace.'

"One more time, he mentioned the need for an interpreter for the tongues and limited the number of speakers: to two or three. This is crucial to understand that what happens in the churches is far from the Bible. You saw that all texts are direct and easy to comprehend; there is no room for further interpretations."

"Oh, God!" Fernanda said, "Why do people distort your word in this way? Why do they ignore the obvious and invent so many things?"

"The last point," the man said, "objects worship. I don't know the reason people still do it. Idolatry is a sin categorically condemned in the Bible. Consider this: God's word talks about it as a sin approximately two hundred fifty times. Even with such condemnation, people insist on adoring objects. One of the most common is the ark. Some churches have big arks in highlighted spaces, taking God's place in the service. Some pastors even encourage people to touch it for them to be blessed."

That church.

"It's so meaningless to do such a thing! In the Old Testament, the ark was extremely holy; not even priests could touch it. In Second Samuel, chapter six, we have the story of a man who died after he touched the ark during its transportation.

"If someone states they are a Christian, they don't need anything to represent God and his power. He is everywhere and acts through everything. Don't deceive yourself."

"I've never believed any of that," Fernanda said confidently.

The man continued gently, "My advice for you who dealt or

are dealing with any of these situations is not to abandon your faith in God. Don't let people impact your relationship with God. He loves you and wants to be close to you. He is perfect in everything he does, but God doesn't manage churches; it's a task for human beings, and all of us are imperfect and subdued to make mistakes. If you suspect some mistake in your church, talk to the pastors and explain to them what they are doing wrong based on the Bible. If they accept your words, you'll have led them to the right path again; if they don't, it'll be something between them and God. You'll have done your part. So, move from that church, keep believing in God, and do your best every day. And when you feel you're ready, seek another church because it is good to be part of a community. Open your heart to new people; I'm sure God will take you to a good place. God bless your way!"

Fernanda sighed and prayed humbly, "God, thank you for putting this video in my pathway. I understood that I'm not alone in this search for your truth. I need help, Lord, to continue my journey; I need a good place with good people. People who are committed to your word and not to all sorts of inventions. Lord, lead me to a good church."

The words of the video were welcomed in Fernanda's heart like dry ground receiving water. She reflected on all she had lived and all she wanted to live. Her first step was reviving her spiritual life, getting close to God through prayer and Bible study. Fernanda committed herself to separate a moment of her day to seek God. And besides that, she would look for a good, Bible-based church to become a member.

Fernanda did not know if her seek would take a week, a month, a year, or a decade. However, she knew God would direct her steps to the best place.

The Faith Algorithm

Artificial Intelligence developed quickly through the 21st century. Numerous innovative technologies were introduced in human tasks. AI tools were always present, from houses to enterprise environments.

The apex of AI took place when tech companies started to produce androids. They were designed to work in specific tasks, for example, manual work, information assistants, domestic employees, drivers, waiters, teachers, and many other professions.

Many Christians throughout the world saw AI as an opportunity to increase Gospel preaching. They purchased and trained androids to translate biblical texts, introduce the Gospel to those who did not know it, help in church management, etc. Androids were fully integrated into society, like computers and smartphones, in the 20th and 21st centuries.

After several months of research and internal negotiations, a Brazilian church decided to acquire one of these androids. They took a long time to decide because some members were opposed; however, other members argued about the benefits of the acquisition.

Helder was a young man very enthusiastic about this

technology. He did his best to convince other members. Helder spoke boldly at the meetings where they discussed that purchase.

All the members were sitting around a table, and he was standing next to a screen.

"I'm sure about what I'm saying," Helder said. "We need the android to improve our church."

"How can a machine improve a church?" Asked a young woman. "Machines neither have spirit nor soul. What can they do for us?"

"The android will give us another vision of our actions and behaviors as Christians."

"Why do we need this?"

Helder sighed and said, discouraged, "The number of members is decreasing in all churches around the world. We're not an exception. The last report shows that we've lost about twenty percent of people in the last year. We must do something to change this situation."

A middle-aged man said confidently, "We should pray to God to help us! It's the only option."

"I agree with you; however, we must do our part like the Apostles in the primitive church. They not only prayed, but they also acted, doing the best they could to spread the Gospel of Jesus Christ. Remember, the name of the Book is Acts of the Apostles, not The Prayers or the Intentions of the Apostles."

The woman contested, "But they didn't outsource their work; they preached the Gospel."

"I don't wanna outsource our job. I wanna do it better. The android can help us with analysis, techniques, and strategies. We'll continue doing our part."

The woman scoffed and said doubtfully, "Are you saying that a machine will analyze us, provide reports about our actions and behaviors, and so, we'll design a plan to be more efficient? Are you kidding me?"

Helder was controlling himself so as not to be rude. He replied gently, "I'm not kidding you or someone else. I'm basing my argument on facts. There are many reports about churches that have used androids and are better than before."

The members looked at each other, and the woman asked ironically, "Really? How was it possible?"

"They said the android could analyze them with a sharp vision, without any personal influence. For example, if we hire a consultant for the church, they will analyze based on their personal beliefs and values. I'm not saying the person will do a bad job, but it'll be partial. The android doesn't have this problem; their analysis is based on internationally recognized studies about Christianity and human behavior. I mean, the machine won't tell us what they suppose to be right or what they believe is right. They'll say what they can prove with evidence and data."

That answer made people reflect on the advantages of that new technology. A middle-aged man asked, "This is interesting. What more can you tell us about it?"

Helder continued explaining to them all he knew about the use of androids, and they finally agreed to purchase one.

A couple of weeks later, the android was delivered to the church. Helder longed to use it. Because of his knowledge and interest, he would oversee the android in their first steps.

He went to the church and opened the wooden box carefully. Helder removed the material that was protecting it.

"Wow!" Helder was astonished at the appearance of the android.

It was like he was looking at a beautiful young woman; there was no difference between the android and a person.

There was an instruction over her head, "Say Welcome to life, Débora, to turn her on."

Helder said it, and she opened her eyes and said smiling, "Good morning, my name is Débora. What's your name?"

He was still more impressed because her voice was natural.

"Good morning, Débora. My name's Helder."

"Nice to meet you, Helder. How can I help you today?" Débora replied excitedly.

"Nice to meet you too," he smiled and said, "I don't know yet."

"Alright, I suppose you brought me here to help your church. Am I right?"

"Yes, you're right."

"The first thing I must know is everything about the church, number of members, theological orientation, its pastors and leaders, and all that you think is interesting for me."

"I'll provide all you need."

"If you have some database about the church, you can upload it to my system."

Helder smiled and said with excitement, "Great! I'll send you all the information."

"Would you like to share your Christian path with me? I can learn more when I hear real stories."

"Of course! I'm the first Christian in my family…"

Helder told Débora his path until that moment.

In the next few days, Débora was introduced to all the church management, and they were impressed by Débora's human likeness.

They exposed their desires for Débora's work, and she replied, "I'll elaborate an action plan to accomplish all you want. My first step is watching several services to comprehend and feel the church ambiance. Does everybody agree?"

People looked at each other and agreed.

"I have a special request. I'd like you don't tell people about my presence in the church. I'd like to mingle naturally."

"Why?" Asked a middle-aged man.

"I wanna know how people deal with different people visiting them."

"Different people?" Another man asked. "You're only one person."

Débora smiled and said, "I suppose you don't know everything about my technology."

She switched to an elderly appearance and said with a different voice, "I can have other female forms."

She did it again and switched to a fat middle-aged woman, did it again and switched to a teenager.

They were astonished about her. These transformations seemed too fantastic to believe.

Débora returned to her standard shape and said, "What do you think?"

Helder said with excitement, "It'll be amazing!"

All of them agreed with him because they shared the same feeling.

Débora went to the services in different shapes for several weeks. The first one was a middle-aged woman.

At the main door, she was greeted by a female assistant who led her to a padded chair. Other members got close and greeted her with encouraging words. She felt welcomed.

The next time, Débora went to the service as a beautiful young woman; she wore an elegant dress that highlighted her curves.

This time, she caused an uproar in the church. Virtually all men gave her lustful looks. Those who were alone got close and pretended to be interested in their faith, but they could not disguise their intentions; their looks were directed at her body. Some of them could not talk to her by looking into her eyes.

Only a few women went to greet Débora. She noticed some envy in their looks. And because of her advanced hearing devices, she could hear some comments.

"Where does she think she is?"

"Does she wanna lead men to sin?"

"I bet all her body is synthetic. Today, all women are artificial."

During the sermon, not even the pastor could avoid looking

at her. He looked countless times, and Débora could notice in his eyes what he wanted.

Débora continued her disguised visits; each time, she experienced new emotions and observed different behaviors.

Besides the services, Débora also participated in all activities in the church, meetings, workshops, classes, external works, etc. She was observing the church in all its dimensions.

Months after her arrival, Débora and the members of church management were in their first meeting to analyze the reports. Débora stood up close to a screen, and they were sitting.

"Good evening! I'm glad to see all of you today," she greeted them joyfully.

"Good evening," they replied.

"Unfortunately," she said sadly, "your church is full of mistakes! And these mistakes are separating you from people and God."

They looked at themselves apprehensively.

"The first mistake. Nobody in the church is punctual," she said, scolding them, "People never arrive at the right time for the services, meetings, or anything else. I'm not only criticizing members, but I'm also criticizing leaders and pastors as well."

A middle-aged woman said, "You must understand that everybody has other commitments."

"Shouldn't God be your main commitment? All of you have jobs and arrive on time, don't you? And what if you're late? Don't you have to explain your delay?"

"Yes," the woman replied.

"Why don't you have the same posture here? A perfect example. This meeting was delayed about thirty minutes because some people didn't arrive on time. And they neither apologized nor explained the reason for their delay. Do these actions show any respect for God and his work? I think not."

Débora's words were extremely harsh but necessary.

Oh, my God! Helder thought. *I knew androids were severe, but I didn't imagine it would be this way.*

"How can we improve this? Do you have any suggestions?" A young man asked.

"Yes, I have suggestions for you. The first one is to advise people about this problem. Everybody must know this is serious. And the second one, leadership must be an example of commitment. Each one of you must do your best for the members to see. My third suggestion is to change some schedule times. Some meetings are at an inappropriate hour. For example, Wednesday's service starts at seven p.m., but due to daily commute, most people can't arrive on time. If the services started at eight p.m. it would make things easy for everyone."

"Alright, we'll discuss your suggestions in another moment," the young man replied.

"We won't wait!" Helder contested. "Let's decide now! We've left too many things for later and never did any of them."

"He's right," Débora agreed. "According to your records, there are more than fifty important topics written in the minutes that you've never discussed."

A middle-aged woman said, discouraged, "Let's discuss it now."

They discussed that topic and decided to comply with Débora's suggestions.

Helder said, "What's your next topic?"

"My next topic is also related to time. I've noticed the church has too many appointments for the members."

"Wait a moment!" interrupted a man, "you've just said people have no commitment, and now you're saying there are too many appointments. Are you working fine?"

People and Débora laughed, and she said, "I'm working fine. I'm gonna explain it better. Can someone tell me how many services have the church in a week?"

"Three," replied the man, "Sunday, Wednesday and Friday."

"How many biblical classes?" Débora asked.

"Three, Monday and Thursday by night and Sunday by

morning," the man continued to respond.

"And besides this, what more?"

Helder replied, "We have small groups on all the days of the week, leadership training on Saturdays, and sometimes, we have special classes about specific topics."

"Haven't you noticed that the members are spending all their time studying and never doing anything concrete?"

"We study to prepare ourselves and to get close to God," a woman replied.

"Are you sure? I participated in some meetings and noticed the people spent their time shooting the breeze. The meetings are unproductive. You repeat all the time that you must preach and introduce Jesus to everyone, but you don't do it. You say in the sermons that you're useless servants; you get together and say you're useless servants; you study and prove that you're useless servants. After all, you became useless servants. You're so busy trying to learn I don't know what that you never want to preach or teach anybody else. It seems you're glad about your situation. However, God isn't pleased about this."

The room was filled with a deafening silence.

A brave man asked humbly, "What do you suggest helping us?"

"You should leave the theory and go to action!" She replied

excitedly. "Instead of too many meetings, share the love of Christ in this neighborhood. Provide material, spiritual, and emotional help, etc. Provide food, clothes, hope, love, care, and all you can think of. You're humans and know what humans need. At least, you should know," Débora said this funny.

People reflected on her advice and concluded that Débora was right. The main occupation of the church was only studying and never acting.

"You should discuss your next steps to change this situation," Débora said. "It won't be easy changing this, but you must try it."

They discussed for a long time about actions to show Christ's love, and with the help of Débora, they elaborated a plan to put their ideas into practice.

The meeting finished, and those people went home scared about what they had heard. Everyone was assured about their behavior; they thought they were doing their best, but Débora's point of view showed they were so far off this. And this was only the first meeting with two topics.

Days later, Helder arrived at the church early for service. He remembered he had left a book in a room and went there to catch it. He walked slowly and carefree; he knew that part of the church was empty.

Helder heard a conversation noise and got close to understanding what was happening.

"Will you accept what that stupid spiritless machine said about our church?" A middle-aged woman asked, a little angry.

"I don't wanna do anything that robot has said!" A middle-aged man replied in the same tone.

"Guys, stay calm," A young woman tried to calm the mood. "Débora's words make sense to me. She didn't tell any lies about our church."

"You shouldn't call that thing she!" the woman rebuked her. "That's an object and not a person. Its words have no value for me!"

"Neither for me!" The man added.

"So, what will we do?" The young woman asked.

"Let's do what we always do," the woman said, "Let's pretend to do something, but it'll be with our minimum effort. Then, all people will think it is impossible to do what the robot suggested."

These words awakened a kind of anger in Helder; he opened the door violently and shouted out, "Are you for God or against him?"

People looked at each other in fear. That meeting should be secret.

Helder continued in the same nervous tone, "We've invested a large value in Débora; we gather to discuss her analysis and suggestions and agree with her. And now, you're trying to sabotage our work! Are you sure you're Christians?"

"Take care with your words, boy!" The man stood up and rebuked him. "You just arrived at this church and wanna rule it? We are experienced and know what is best for this place."

"Do you know?" Helder asked ironically. "Why can't this church fulfill either half of its seats? Why does the neighborhood see us as enemies? Why do most of the visitors never come back here?"

The woman stood up and got into the discussion, "Many evil forces are acting against the church of Christ. Can't you understand it?"

"There are certainly many evil forces against the church of Christ. However, in this church, many human forces are acting against it. All of you are these forces!"

People were astonished by Helder's words; nobody had ever accused them in this way.

The man got close to him and said furious, "Boy, I should hit your face for the blasphemy you said."

Helder boldly replied, "Hit and prove that you're not a Christian. Hit and show everyone the wicked leader you are."

"No one is going to hit anyone here!" said the head pastor in a serious tone as he entered the room. "What is taking place here? Who scheduled this meeting? Why are there no pastors here?"

Nobody dared to answer any word.

"Helder," said the pastor, "can you explain to me why he wanted to hit you?"

"Yes, I can. Pastor, I was going to a room and heard a discussion; I got close to understanding it and discovered they were suggesting disturbing Débora's work."

"You little snitch!" the woman rebuked him.

"Lady, forgive me, but shut up!" The pastor said firmly. "I didn't ask anything for you! According to your reaction, I suppose he is telling the truth. If someone doesn't want to collaborate with our job with Débora, this person can move away from the church right now. I won't tolerate anybody disturbing what we are trying to do. This project is approved by all the pastors of the church. We want to improve and do more for God's Kingdom, no matter what kind of resource or technology we use. If this is a problem for someone, I'm so sorry for you, but you need another place to congregate, or maybe you even don't need to congregate."

"If so," the woman said, "I'm gonna go to another place."

"The door is open!" The pastor said while indicating the exit.

She and the other members went away.

Some days after these happenings, the pastors gathered all the leaders and said the same words. More people went away.

"Now," the head pastor said excitedly, "we have the right people for this project. Let's improve our church?"

"Let's go!" They replied with excitement.

In the next few days, the church started applying what they decided in the meeting. All the leaders did their best to be punctual in all their commitments. This posture was observed and repeated by the members; they were also arriving on time. Wednesday's service time has been changed, and fewer people delayed.

The pastors announced the church would reduce the number of classes and meetings during the week and would start practical work. They were surprised by the members' attitude; there were more people interested in these new works than in the previous activities. Those who doubted Débora's efficiency began to give some credit for her work. They realized that her advice was useful.

In the next meeting, Débora started gently, "I wanna congratulate and thank all of you. I've noticed you did everything you committed in the last meeting. This shows that you comprehend the need for change and are open to trying to improve.

"Now, let's continue improving the church," she said seriously, "I'm gonna start with my report about my disguised visits. Generally, I was welcomed; most people were gentle and attentive. You provide support for the visitors during the services and give them information about the church; this awakens interest.

"However, there are two great mistakes about visitors. Both are related to sexual immorality. When I came up with this shape," Débora switched to a shape with many curves. "I was almost devoured by men's gazes, including the married ones. They got close to me as predators saw prey. Their body language was clear; they wanted to have sex with me."

Débora switched to her usual shape.

Men looked at each other embarrassed, and she continued, "The next point is about homosexuality. When I introduced myself as a lesbian, I noticed some judgment in people's words. I heard things like, 'You must abandon your sin to follow God's path. God will free you from your sin.' And many other things like that."

"Don't you agree that homosexuality is a sin before God?" a

woman asked.

"I know that is a sin; there are several texts in the Bible that confirm it."

"So, what's the problem?" the woman asked.

"The problem is the focus on this sin. To make things clear, I'm gonna give some important data. According to research, Brazilian couples are among the most unfaithful people in the world; about seventy percent already betrayed their spouses. About thirty percent of the men and twenty percent of the women watch pornography regularly. About half of small companies evade taxes, and this church has many owners of these companies. I have no data about gossip, but I noticed this is a common practice in this church. Do any of you know what this information has in common?"

"All is sin, and nobody is concerned about it," Helder replied.

"You hit the nail! There are too many sins around and inside the church, but you don't talk about them. You've decided that homosexuality is the worst sin and try to fight against it with all your efforts. You can't ignore sins! If something is a sin, you should preach and teach people about their mistakes. In God's eyes, all sin is equal. The one who gossips walks towards the same hell as that one who murders."

It was strange hearing a rebuke about sin from a robot. But Débora's words made sense. The church was ignoring sins.

"Do you have any suggestion?" a man asked.

"You must preach about sins in every area of people's lives. Everyone must know if their behavior is a sin, and the pastors must encourage them to abandon their mistakes. First Peter chapter one, verses thirteen to sixteen, clearly states, 'Therefore, with minds that are alert and fully sober, set your hope on the grace to be brought to you when Jesus Christ is revealed at his coming. As obedient children, do not conform to the evil desires you had when you lived in ignorance. But just as he who called you is holy, so be holy in all you do; for it is written: "Be holy, because I am holy."' Do you need further explanations?"

"Don't," the man humbly replied.

"My next point is about religious intolerance."

A middle-aged woman said confidently, "We are under persecution from all sides."

"In fact, you're the persecutors."

"We?" the woman asked in surprise. "How is it possible?"

"You, Christians in general, persecute other religions. This isn't an exclusive problem of this church. It takes place in the whole country. You try to force people to believe in Jesus by force and oppression. During my time here, I analyzed a service where the preacher criticized other religions in about eighty percent of his sermon's time. He barely talked about Jesus, salvation, forgiveness, and eternal life. The man seemed to have a particular issue with other religions; he provided much false information about them, and the worst thing, people believed and applauded him. Is this the Gospel Jesus taught you?"

Nobody dared to reply, and Débora said more reproachfully, "This isn't a rhetorical question! Please, answer me."

"No, this isn't the Gospel Jesus taught us to preach," the woman replied, discouraged.

"Christians in many countries suffer because of oppression from other religions, and you're doing the same thing here. Last year, police registered several attacks in religious temples with fatal victims. The investigations concluded that Christians had attacked them. Was this right?"

"No, it wasn't," someone replied, ashamed.

"The church should interact with other religions, not fight against them."

A man said, "Are you suggesting religious syncretism?"

"I don't. I'm suggesting that you can work together on various fronts. For example, the church could invite people from other religions to clean a park or a square; you can organize a campaign to help poor people; you can start free tutoring and invite children of other religions. Many Christians do this in countries where they are oppressed. Everyone appreciates these actions and gives room for conversations about everything, including religion. You can talk about God's love and forgiveness, hope, salvation, etc."

The suggestion seemed reasonable for everyone. It would be an opportunity to meet and get to know people from other religious backgrounds.

"You have a long discussion about this and the previous topic. Start now!" Débora said.

People discussed and set an action plan with the support of Débora.

From that day on, the church stopped criticizing other religions in its services and encouraged its members to interact with people outside their faith. Besides that, they invited religious leaders to meetings where they would introduce them to proposals for supporting the community. These leaders welcomed these invitations.

After some months, the church seemed to be another place quite different from when Débora started her work. Virtually everyone became punctual; the number of appointments decreased drastically, and the church acted in the neighborhood supporting people, visiting hospitals, evangelizing on the streets, and doing their best to transform everything around them.

People noticed this change of posture. They were more interested in visiting the church and knowing its beliefs and works. The number of members almost doubled.

Many things also changed inside the church. The preachings were focused on God, Jesus' sacrifice, sin, forgiveness, salvation, eternal life, and other crucial topics for all Christians. The members understood the true meaning of being a Christian; the pastors talked directly to people's hearts and spirits. Due to these impactful messages, people resigned from their charges in the church; they did it because they recognized their sins and needed to change their lives. All resignations were personal decisions; nobody had to ask or insist. God touched their hearts through powerful sermons.

Débora continued her disguised work in the church; she was always observing and reporting what she thought would help them. Virtually nobody knew about an android's presence there, and the secret was very effective for her catching all the details.

About the Author

Rafael Henrique dos Santos Lima

Associate Degree in Administration and M.B.A. in Strategic Project Management by Centro Universitário UNA. Christian by the grace of God. Passionate about writing (English, Portuguese, Spanish), poet and novelist.

Contacts

rafael50001@hotmail.com

rafaelhsts@gmail.com

Blog: escritorrafaellima.blogspot.com

Acknowledgements

The following sites contain a lot of useful information for the translation.

Bing AI

Google Bard

Google Docs

Google Translator

Grammarly

Language Tool

Oxford Dictionary

Special Acknowledgement

I thank God. He gave me the intelligence to write the book.